KID CONFIDENT

#2

How to Master
Your Mood
in Middle School

KID CONFIDENT #2

How to Master
Your Mood
in Middle School

by Lenka Glassman, PsyD   illustrated by DeAndra Hodge

Magination Press · Washington, DC · American Psychological Association

Emma—my baby girl, thank you for being such a happy, loving, sparkly, strong, and sparkling human. I love you beyond words, no matter what. And to my amazing, brave, resilient, smart, capable, and insightful clients—thank you for inspiring and challenging me every day. It is such an honor to be a part of your journeys—LG

To my mom and big brother for their love and support—DH

**Books for Kids From the
American Psychological Association**

Copyright © 2022 by Lenka Glassman. Illustrations copyright © 2022 by DeAndra Hodge. Published in 2022 by Magination Press, an imprint of the American Psychological Association.

Magination Press is a registered trademark of the American Psychological Association. Order books at maginationpress.org or call 1-800-374-2721.

Series editor: Bonnie Zucker, PsyD

Book design by Rachel Ross

Printed by Lake Book Manufacturing, Inc., Melrose Park, IL

Library of Congress Cataloging-in-Publication Data
Names: Glassman, Lenka, author. | Hodge, DeAndra, illustrator.
Title: Kid confident #2: how to master your mood in middle school / by Lenka Glassman, PhD; illustrations by DeAndra Hodge.
Description: Washington, DC: Magination Press, [2022] | Includes bibliographical references. | Summary: "Middle schoolers learn how to identify, manage, and self regulate their emotions and moods"—Provided by publisher.
Identifiers: LCCN 2022007768 (print) | LCCN 2022007769 (ebook) | ISBN 9781433838187 (hardback) | ISBN 9781433838194 (ebook)
Subjects: LCSH: Mood (Psychology) in adolescence—Juvenile literature. | Emotions in adolescence—Juvenile literature. | Mood (Psychology)—Juvenile literature. | Emotions—Juvenile literature.
Classification: LCC BF724.3.M64 G53 2022 (print) | LCC BF724.3.M64 (ebook) | DDC 152.4—dc23/eng/20220325
LC record available at https://lccn.loc.gov/2022007768
LC ebook record available at https://lccn.loc.gov/2022007769

Manufactured in the United States of America

10 9 8 7 6 5 4 3 2 1

CONTENTS

Dear Reader (Don't Skip This!)

It's likely that you've heard the words "mood" and "emotion" before, and you probably recognize what it's like to feel happy, comfortable, and joyful, or down, angry, and frustrated. You may even know the external situations, people, and events that have the power to create these emotional experiences inside of you. When you're in a positive mood, you feel great, and life seems easy, hopeful, and fun. When you're in a bad mood, everything can feel awful, and life seems hopeless and so hard.

With so much going on in your life, between friends, academic stress, family drama, and all the transitions that happen at your age (personal life, school, and even changes in your body), it's easy to feel like you have no control over your mood and emotions. The truth is, you have a lot more power inside of you than you can imagine. You can take control in a way that leaves you feeling balanced and empowered no matter what life throws your way. When you learn strategies to shift your internal experience, you'll feel even better when things are going well in your life. More importantly though, when you learn to **MASTER YOUR MOOD**, you'll feel balanced, strong, steady, and confident, even when things in your life are really hard and nothing is going your way.

- Imagine what it would be like to face the challenges in your life head on and with a sense of confidence and grace.

- Imagine if you could turn around a recent stressful situation and actually feel a sense of peace about it!

- Imagine what it would be like to experience positive accomplishments, events, and relationships with even more excitement, instead of waiting for the "other shoe to drop."

Sounds amazing right? It may seem out of reach right now, but trust me, anyone can master these skills and find their zen, **EVEN YOU!** I bet that as a middle schooler, you are familiar, even too familiar, with bad moods and difficult emotions. I wrote this book specifically for YOU! Middle school life is full of changes, surprises, curve balls, and challenges. If you've been feeling overwhelmed by the drama, harshness, and intense emotions, you're not alone. This book will give you the power to get through it all and land on your feet. By the end of this book, you will learn just how to manage your mood and emotions, and trust me, you will feel **UNSTOPPABLE**.

*I*n this book, I'll help you understand your emotional experiences and mood in a new way and help you feel so much lighter and more confident about yourself and your future. We'll take it step by step and break things down into small sections so you can read a little at a time and feel like you're getting somewhere.

Overachiever? Be my guest and read the whole book at once! If you're anything like I was when I was your age, I'm guessing you probably aren't thrilled to be reading a self-help book, or maybe even any book at all. I promise this book will be different. No matter what style of learner you are, no matter what you are facing in your life, there will be something in this book that you will be glad you learned. Not everyone nerds out on mood regulation skills like me— so I've included lots of graphics, illustrations, mantras, and prompts to keep things fresh and not boring!

Here are a few things you will master while reading this book:

- Staying cool and calm during really tough moments
- Feeling in charge of your reactions in all types of situations

- Feeling happier overall, and being able to see the positives in your life more easily
- Being alone with your thoughts and not feeling so down and lonely
- Having more energy for your day and the things that matter to you the most
- Knowing that you can handle anything that life throws your way
- Picking yourself back up when you fall apart (or when your life does!)
- Feeling even better about the best parts of your life

Will you be able to use these skills perfectly every single day, with every single challenge? I consider myself a total master of my mood, and even I can't do that. Will you learn to rise to the challenge of creating a more Zen energy enough of the time to make a big difference in your overall well-being? Absolutely!

This book is divided into 10 chapters. The first half of the book will give you the scoop on why mood struggles in middle school are so common and intense **(SPOILER ALERT: IT'S NORMAL!)**. If you're curious about your brain and how your mood is created, the first section of this book is for you!

In the second half of the book, you will learn about four main aspects of your mood, how they work, and most importantly, what to do to take charge and feel better. You'll learn how to shift your body, thinking, emotions, and actions with concrete, easy-to-use strategies.

Also included is a bunch of **EXTRA INFO** like:

Fun Facts— Surprising information about topics related to each chapter.

Take a Minute— Self-reflection activities and questions for you to ponder. Take a minute to pause, reflect, and think about a particular skill or concept being discussed.

A Call to Action— Specific strategies to help soothe, relax, or energize your body, shift your perspective, accept and calm your emotions, and take active steps that will leave you feeling more balanced, grounded, and happy.

Grab a Pen— Writing exercises for you to reflect and get your thoughts out and down on paper and write down major points, like a cheat sheet of the most helpful pieces of the book that you can have with you everywhere, and are specific to YOU.

Pro Tip— Direct messages from me meant to learn, inspire, help, and motivate.

Take-Away— At the end of each chapter, you will have this section that ties everything together.

Throughout the book you will also get to read real life examples of kids just like you, who overcame their mood struggles and came out on top. Don't worry, I'll tell you exactly how they got there!

Once you learn to manage your mood:

You will feel lighter and life will feel easier.

You will take setbacks in stride.

You will bounce back when things don't go your way.

You will navigate conflicts in your relationships with more grace.

You will feel a deeper sense of confidence.

You will see your future as full of possibilities even during tough moments.

Sound too good to be true? The truth is, life has hard moments, and I can't change that for you. What I can help you change is your relationship with yourself and with your circumstances. This book will help you get there, no matter what your starting point is. I promise I've put every ounce of knowledge, experience, and love that I have into making this book as helpful as it can be. All you need to bring to the table is a willingness to try, a desire to feel better, and a commitment to yourself to open the book one chapter or page at a time. I'll guide you through fun activities, illustrations, and strategies designed to help you get the most out of the information you will learn.

—Lenka G.

A Note for the Adults in Your Life

$\mathcal{A}$s a child and teen psychologist, I see many parents who come to my office at their wits' end with their child's mood. In my experience, middle school is one of the most difficult time periods for both children and parents. Just last week, a parent walked into my office exclaiming, "If I just breathe the wrong way, my daughter's mood gets set off." Your child's mood can impact your entire family atmosphere and leave a trail of stress, tension, pain, and conflict. Worst of all, a bad mood and trouble managing difficult emotions can make it more difficult to feel close with your child. Over time, the energy in your home can take a nosedive into persistent negativity and detachment.

Where is the little human that laughed, smiled, asked for hugs, and told you about their day? Where is the child who always wanted to have family game night? Where is the happy, relaxed, and sweet kiddo who you used to know? Let me tell you, they are still there, just veiled with the tremendous physical, social, and academic challenges they are facing at this age. Every child is different, and while some seemingly sail through their middle school years, others seem to get stuck on a rollercoaster of up and down moods that can humble even the most insightful, loving, and knowledgeable parent.

Do you wish you could talk to your child about their mood and behavior in a way that is constructive? Do you want to help your child see things from different perspectives? Do you desperately wish for the overall mood in your house to be more positive? You are not alone. Middle school is tough for everyone involved. There is a reason why there are so many shows, movies, memes, and jokes focused on the middle school experience. It really can be that intense.

This book is here to help you and your middle-schooler navigate the ups and downs of middle school with confidence and compassion so that you can come out feeling grounded, empowered, and with an even closer bond. Your child may not be asking for help, or even seem interested in connecting with you about their mood. This is very common. At this age, they want to be able to focus on their social relationships and on forming their identity without a lot of interference from their parents. Even though they may resist your support, they desperately need guidance, validation, and structure to handle all of their new independence in healthy ways.

Your child wants what we all want: to be seen, understood, and loved. My hope is for this book to bridge that gap and allow you and your child to sit down and learn together in a way that is meaningful and deeply impactful. I've included easy-to-read information to help you and your child better understand the mood shifts and emotional experiences of middle school, as well as many examples, activities, and easy-to-implement strategies to help your child feel confident navigating the ups and downs of life not just in middle school, but throughout the rest of their lives.

Your presence, connection, and understanding are invaluable to your tween or teen. Helping your child understand their mood, validating their experience, opening the lines of communication, and helping them use the strategies outlined in this book will go a long way towards helping them grow into successful, resilient, and confident adults. *I'm cheering you on!*

—Lenka Glassman, PsyD

chapter 1

All About Mood

ver been in a bad mood and didn't even know why? What's the difference between an emotion and a mood? How does your brain affect your mood, and your mood affect your brain? How do your life circumstances and daily habits affect your mood?

Turns out, I have answers to these questions! Or at least, I have some ideas. I'll talk about all of the areas that can have a major impact on how you feel, like the **mood feedback cycle**, which includes how your body feels, how you think, how you manage your emotions, and which actions you chose to take. And of course, your mood is affected by some life circumstances that you may have control over, like sleep, nutrition, and movement, and things you have no control over, like pain, mental or physical illness, or loss.

As you begin reading, imagine how you want to feel on a daily basis. What would it be like to feel more in control of your emotions, reactions, and mood? How would your life and your relationships be different? How do you want to feel about yourself after reading each chapter? Keep this idea in mind as you read.

So what *is* the difference between an emotion and mood?

EMOTION

A moment in time

 A short time

Immediate response to a person, thought, event, or action

Frequently changes from moment to moment

Gives us info about ourselves

Is data to help us make choices

VS. MOOD

Overall emotional vibe

Lasts for days, weeks, months

A state of mind

Created by our:

- biology
- feedback cycles of thoughts, emotions, & actions
- life circumstances
- daily habits

To Do:

When we talk about a **feeling** or **emotion**, we usually mean an intense, in-the-moment experience that tends to last for a short time. An emotion is typically an immediate response to a particular event, person, thought, or action. Our emotions often change from moment to moment and impact the decisions we make. For example, if we feel joy while doing an activity, like playing soccer, that emotion becomes information that we use to make the decision to try out for the school soccer team. If we feel sad most of the time around a certain group of friends, that emotion might factor in to the decision to put a lot of effort (or not!) into those friendships.

Along with our bodies and thoughts, emotions are an important source of information we can use to navigate our lives. You will learn much more about your emotions and how they play a role in your mood in Chapter 5, but for now just know that each of us responds to emotions differently, has a different threshold for intense emotions, and our ability to manage these emotions (called **self-regulation**) varies.

A FEELING OR EMOTION USUALLY MEANS AN INTENSE IN-THE-MOMENT EXPERIENCE THAT TENDS TO LAST FOR A SHORT TIME.

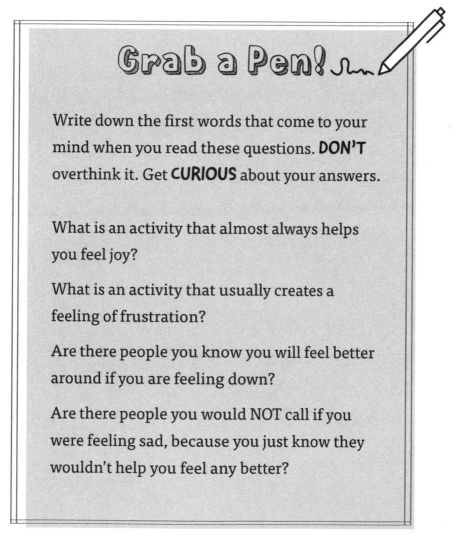

Grab a Pen!

Write down the first words that come to your mind when you read these questions. **DON'T** overthink it. Get **CURIOUS** about your answers.

What is an activity that almost always helps you feel joy?

What is an activity that usually creates a feeling of frustration?

Are there people you know you will feel better around if you are feeling down?

Are there people you would NOT call if you were feeling sad, because you just know they wouldn't help you feel any better?

Our **mood** is our overall emotional experience over time and can last days, weeks, or even months. This is an important distinction—mood is your **OVERALL VIBE** and the energy you bring to your life. Our mood affects every part of our lives—how we feel about ourselves, our relationships with others, and even our physical and mental health. Our mood depends on a few different things, not just a specific event or moment. Our mood is affected by internal factors like our biology (hormones and brain chemicals), psychology (personality and learned responses), life circumstances that we have no choice in (like an injury or illness), and daily habits that are within our control (like sleep and movement).

YOUR MOOD IS YOUR OVERALL VIBE THAT LASTS FOR DAYS, WEEKS, OR EVEN MONTHS.

Another way to look at the difference is seeing our mood as a particular **STATE OF MIND**, and an emotion as a particular **MOMENT IN TIME**. While an emotion can influence how we choose to act in a given moment, or respond to a concrete situation, our mood has a wider reach, impacting the way we feel on a daily basis.

 # How is your mood created?

 ...WITH YOUR BRAIN! I'll talk more about the nitty gritty of your brain and its role in your mood in Chapter 3, but in general, the way your brain is structured, and the way it communicates via hormones and neurochemicals, is critical to how you feel. In particular, the brain area linked to thinking and reasoning (the prefrontal cortex) is thought to be less active when your mood is down, while the area linked to emotion processing (the limbic system) is super active.

Another way of saying this is that when you're in a negative mood, your "**feeling brain**" is more active than your "**thinking brain,**" and these two parts of your neurobiological system are not communicating very well.

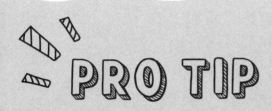

PRO TIP

We don't usually refer to emotions as positive or negative. Emotions are neither good nor bad and are totally normal to have, but of course some are uncomfortable to experience and are a pain to deal with. So in this book we'll be using the term "positive mood" and "negative mood" to describe states of mind.

Your body's sensations, thoughts, emotions, and actions are all the psychological factors that make up your mood. These all work together to create a feedback cycle that can either keep you stuck in a super bummer place or keep you solidly in Zen mode.

In order to gain mastery over your mood, first you need to know what these cycles look like.

When someone is focused on helpful, calm thoughts and moving their body in an energetic way, they will feel pleasant emotions, and take positive actions. This will create a positive mood that keeps going. When someone is focused on negative thoughts, their body feels heavy and slow. Their emotions are challenging, it's difficult to take any helpful actions, and their mood will be negative.

In turn, the type of mood we are in impacts our body, thoughts, emotions, and actions in ways that keep that particular mood going and going!

This means that when someone is in a good mood, it has a positive impact on their body, their thoughts, their emotions, and their actions. This creates a feedback cycle that keeps their good mood consistent. And when someone's mood is really down, they often get caught in a feedback cycle that's not so helpful because of the way their body feels, how they are thinking, what they are feeling, and the actions they are choosing. **IT CAN BE A BIT OF A VICIOUS CYCLE!**

Our mood is

E-V-E-R-Y-

T-H-I-N-G!

MOOD CYCLE: HOW IT WORKS

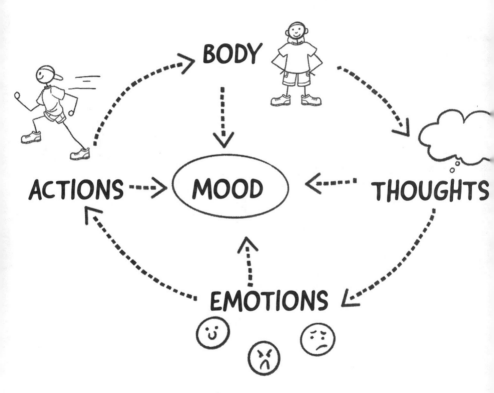

This is the basic cycle and shows how your mood is influenced by your emotions, body language, actions, and thinking.

NEGATIVE MOOD CYCLE

Now that you know the basics, let's take a look at how a negative or down mood could look in real life and what might result because of it!

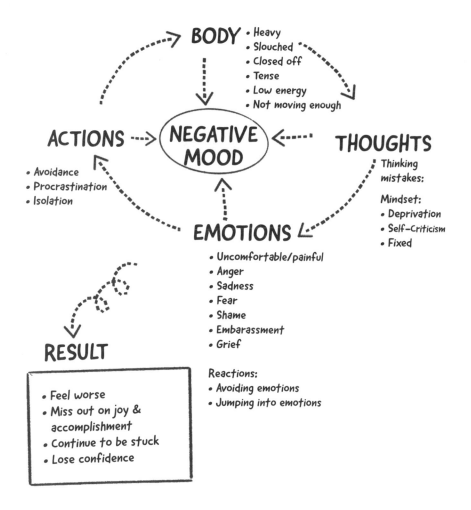

BODY
• Heavy
• Slouched
• Closed off
• Tense
• Low energy
• Not moving enough

NEGATIVE MOOD

ACTIONS
• Avoidance
• Procrastination
• Isolation

THOUGHTS
Thinking mistakes:

Mindset:
• Deprivation
• Self-Criticism
• Fixed

EMOTIONS
• Uncomfortable/painful
• Anger
• Sadness
• Fear
• Shame
• Embarassment
• Grief

Reactions:
• Avoiding emotions
• Jumping into emotions

RESULT
• Feel worse
• Miss out on joy & accomplishment
• Continue to be stuck
• Lose confidence

MEET MARIA. Maria, who usually got As and Bs in her classes, had been struggling in her math course. She had a new teacher this year and just

MARIA (she/her)

wasn't understanding the concepts as quickly as she usually does. For her midterm exam, she worked really hard and spent hours preparing. When she got a C-, her mood tumbled down and kept going. Let's take a closer look at how the negative mood cycle played out for Maria and how she took steps to get herself unstuck.

NEGATIVE MOOD AND THE BODY: When you are in a bad mood, your body feels heavy, tired, and tense. You may carry yourself in a slouched, closed off, and tight posture. This type of body language gives people the impression that you are unfriendly or want to be alone. You probably don't even realize this! People may not respond to you or approach you as easily, which leaves you feeling worse, right?

What do you notice in your body when you are feeling down or annoyed?

Maria noticed that her chest felt heavy, she had a knot in her stomach, was avoiding eye contact, and did not want to do anything at all. So what did Maria do?

- Practiced calm breathing in class until the heaviness in her chest subsided.

- Went for a walk right after school to "cool off."

NEGATIVE MOOD AND THINKING: When you're in a bad mood, you may tend to think in ways that are unhelpful, and sometimes even unreasonable. You notice all of the negatives around you, and barely notice any positives. When this happens, you are likely making thinking mistakes, also known as "cognitive distortions," and they keep your mood and confidence way down. These ways of thinking can create a hopeless and self-critical mindset (your overall view of yourself, others, and life).

Lots of unhelpful thoughts popped up in Maria's head that she challenged with more helpful thoughts, like this:

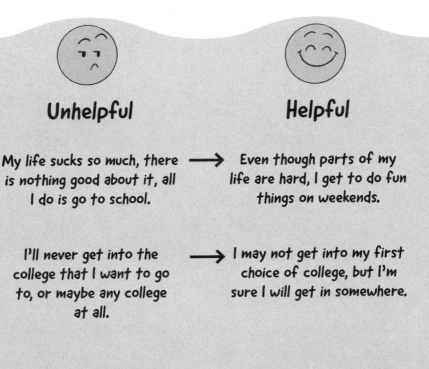

Unhelpful

My life sucks so much, there is nothing good about it, all I do is go to school.

I'll never get into the college that I want to go to, or maybe any college at all.

I'm just such a failure, I should have studied more.

My friends don't even care. Who needs friends anyway.

Helpful

Even though parts of my life are hard, I get to do fun things on weekends.

I may not get into my first choice of college, but I'm sure I will get in somewhere.

I tried my best to be prepared, and I'll get another chance next time.

I have several good friends that care about me, even if it doesn't always seem like it.

What are some <u>unhelpful</u> thoughts that pop into your head when you're in a negative mood? What do you wish you could think to yourself instead?

NEGATIVE MOOD AND EMOTIONS: When you are stuck in a negative mindset and thinking negative thoughts, you can feel sad, angry, frustrated, and unhappy. You experience a lot of emotions that are uncomfortable, and sometimes even painful.

Maria had lots of emotions in the moment, and some even came up in her body much later as she thought about that day. Some of them were sadness, anger, hopelessness, dread, and shame. Maria was so uncomfortable and wanted the emotions to just go away. What did Maria do with these emotions instead?

- Maria noticed her feelings without trying to avoid OR fully jump into them.

- She thought of her favorite mantra:
  "I will NOT die from a feeling!"

NEGATIVE MOOD AND ACTIONS: When your body, thoughts, and emotions are negative, your actions go along with them. It is hard to take actions that might help you feel joy or accomplishment, like reaching out to a friend, going for a walk, or starting on your homework. Sometimes, you might even avoid doing the very things that would help you get back on track.

Maria's instinct was to get away and ignore all of her friends' texts and calls after class. Because Maria missed the invite, her friends all went out for ice cream without her. She felt even worse when she saw a photo of them on social media. What do you think Maria did to get unstuck? It was hard **BUT:**

- Maria texted her best friend Christina and explained how she felt about the test.

- Maria felt so much more connected and balanced than she had all day.

- Maria made a plan to hang out with Christina that weekend, which helped her relax and get through the day.

Go Maria!

 Has a friend of yours ever ignored you when they have had a really rough day? Have you ever avoided people when you were feeling down?

As you can see, even though Maria couldn't change her exam grade, she had the power to shift her mood in a major way just by taking active steps to move, think, manage her emotions, and act differently.

I hope Maria's story will help you see how **THIS IS 100% POSSIBLE IN YOUR LIFE TOO!** Though it didn't make her mood instantly perfect, Maria felt a lot more confident and even proud of herself for being able to understand how she could start to help herself feel better. You can learn how to do the same!

Take a Minute!

Do you know what area of the mood cycle you tend to get stuck in? For lots of people, taking a helpful action when in a bad mood is really hard. For some though, "thinking" differently is an even greater challenge. Think about where you get stuck.

It's important to know that although we play a part in the negative mood cycle, it's not something we do on purpose, and **THERE IS NO ROOM FOR SELF-BLAME OR CRITICISM HERE.** Self-blame will only make things worse. Now you know there is a way out!

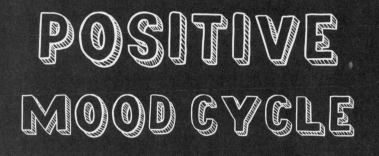

POSITIVE MOOD CYCLE

Now your mood isn't always negative or down, right? Here's how a positive mood could look like in real life and what might result because of it!

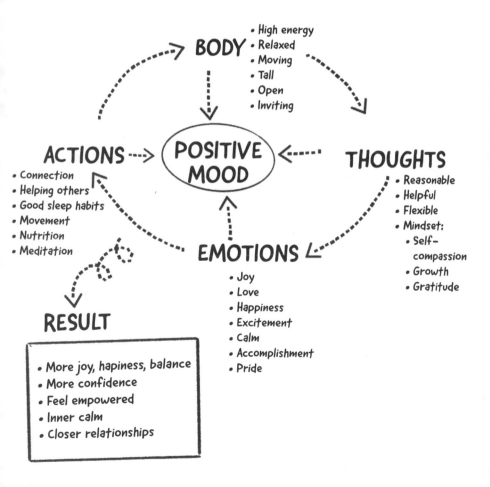

BODY
- High energy
- Relaxed
- Moving
- Tall
- Open
- Inviting

POSITIVE MOOD

THOUGHTS
- Reasonable
- Helpful
- Flexible
- Mindset:
  - Self-compassion
  - Growth
  - Gratitude

ACTIONS
- Connection
- Helping others
- Good sleep habits
- Movement
- Nutrition
- Meditation

EMOTIONS
- Joy
- Love
- Happiness
- Excitement
- Calm
- Accomplishment
- Pride

RESULT
- More joy, hapiness, balance
- More confidence
- Feel empowered
- Inner calm
- Closer relationships

Positively

A positive mood shows up in our body, our mindset, how we think about things, our emotions, and how we act. Importantly, when our bodies, thoughts, emotions, and actions are positive, others tend to want to connect with us, and they respond to us in positive ways. This is how a positive mood keeps going—it continues to create more opportunities to feel better.

POSITIVE MOOD AND THE BODY: When you are in a good mood, your body feels light, energetic, and relaxed. You tend to carry yourself in a tall, firm, and grounded posture. This type of body language makes people feel relaxed and drawn to you, because you look friendly and inviting. **How does your body feel when you are happy?**

POSITIVE MOOD AND THINKING: When you are in a good mood, you tend to notice all of the positives in yourself and around you. Your mindset is full of gratitude, abundance, self-compassion, and potential

Positive!

for growth. **What is one positive thing that you think about yourself when you are feeling confident?**

POSITIVE MOOD AND EMOTIONS: When you are in a positive mindset and thinking helpful thoughts, you feel hopeful and happy. You experience a lot of emotions that feel good, such as joy, admiration, gratitude, and excitement, just to name a few. **What is your favorite emotion to feel?**

POSITIVE MOOD AND ACTIONS: When your body, thoughts, and emotions are positive, your actions go along with them. You act in a way that is friendly, energetic, open, and curious, and you are motivated to do the things that bring you even more joy and calm. Other people tend to respond to you in a positive way, too, making you feel even better, and continuing to feed the positive mood feedback cycle. **What is an activity that reliably makes you feel joyful or accomplished?**

Just like Maria, you can jump into a positive mood cycle by learning to change your body's energy, think more positively, shift your mindset, master your emotions, and take positive actions.

No better time to start training your brain to create more helpful thoughts about yourself than the present moment. **LIKE. RIGHT. NOW.**

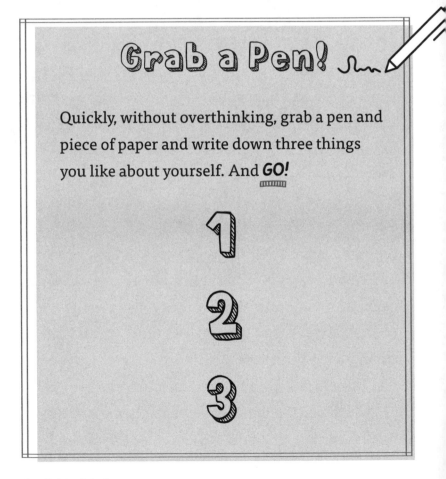

Grab a Pen!

Quickly, without overthinking, grab a pen and piece of paper and write down three things you like about yourself. And *GO!*

1

2

3

If you are like some of the kids I work with, your brain might be having the thought: "I literally don't like anything about myself!" Let me assure you, you are NOT alone. For many people—kids and grown-ups—thinking more compassionately about themselves doesn't come naturally and takes a lot of practice.

Self-confidence and self-compassion "muscles" need to be worked and strengthened just like the physical muscles in our bodies. So, if you feel like this exercise is like trying to run a marathon when you haven't even gone on a walk around the block in forever, try this instead:

- Ask the kindest person you know what three things they love most about you.
- Fake it 'til you make it: write down three positive things you WISH you thought about yourself.
- If you have a pet, ask yourself what three things they would say they love about you (if they could speak).

FACE IT. SOME THINGS YOU CAN'T CONTROL!

In addition to our brain and the feedback cycle, there are a lot of challenges that life can bring our way that we don't have a lot of control over. These can have a major impact on our everyday mood! These can be things like:

- injury or illness

- loss of a family member or friend

- chronic pain

- family struggles

- learning differences or an IEP

- physical or health challenges

- body size or shape

- social injustice, sexism, racism

BUT... SOME THINGS ARE TOTALLY IN YOUR HANDS.

There are so many small daily actions that can have a major impact on your mood and well-being. These daily habits are within your control:

- sleep habits
- movement/physical exercise
- getting outside
- screen use
- social media use
- nutrition
- sports and creative outlets
- connecting with friends & family
- volunteering or doing something kind for others
- being an advocate or ally to others

THE FASTEST WAY TO A BETTER MOOD IS TO MAKE SMALL DAILY CHANGES.

Move!

Z Z z Sleep!

Make a checklist!
☑ ☑ ☑

Call a friend!

IT GETS EASIER THE MORE YOU DO IT.

Take-Away!

Getting stuck in a bad mood for days, weeks, or longer can make you feel hopeless. It's ok to struggle with getting your stride back. That is what this book is for! Just by opening this book and starting to read, you are on your way to learning the skills you need to get unstuck, feel more joy, and experience more ease and wellness in your life.

This book will help you understand and gain power over all of the things that have a major impact on your mood, including:

★ Your brain (both the thinking brain and the feeling brain)

★ Your body, your thoughts, your mindset, your emotions, and your actions

★ Life circumstances that are beyond your control, like illness or injury

★ Daily habits that you do have control over, like sleep and movement

Chapter 2

Big Emotions & Bigger Moods

The truth is, you are dealing with some unique obstacles to achieving a balanced mood and staying cool under the pressure of big feelings right now. There are so many reasons for this! Some of these are completely out of your control (like your brain chemistry or developmental stage), some have to do with school and social demands, and others are related to the choices you make and how you take care of yourself emotionally (sleep, challenging your perfectionism, spending time with friends).

No one is in a good mood all the time. If they look like they are, tell you they are, or appear to be on their social media, they are probably not telling the whole truth! Seriously. Life is full of tough moments, and no one can sail through without ever feeling down or occasionally making decisions that aren't very helpful when intense emotions come up.

Let's be honest: life can be hard, no matter what age you are, but in middle school you are facing a lot of challenges. The **GOOD NEWS** is (remember we want to try to get our brains to generate some positives here) that, now that you know the deal, you have a great comeback when your parents complain about your mood.

LET'S BREAK THIS DOWN A LITTLE. DURING MIDDLE SCHOOL, YOU ARE FACING MANY BIG CHALLENGES. The first challenge is due to biology. The early teen years are some of the toughest in terms of both mood and managing emotions. This skill is called **self-regulation**. I promise things do get better gradually as you enter your later teens and young adulthood. There are a few reasons behind this.

I'll take a deeper dive into how your brain plays a role in your mood in Chapter 3, but basically, the wise "thinking" part of your brain still has a lot of growing to do, while the impulsive "feeling" part of your brain is super active.

Another thing you can blame biology for? Hormone shifts!

Hormones play a major role in how we think and feel, and they go through major shifts during puberty. Not only does this impact how quickly your moods change and how intense your emotional responses are, but it is also behind the many physical changes that your body is going through.

SO, YOUR BRAIN IS CHANGING ON THE INSIDE WHILE YOUR BODY IS CHANGING ON THE OUTSIDE!

Adjusting to a changing and growing body is tough, and even tougher if you are stressed by your body shape and size or not confident about the way you look. If you feel fine and rock in these areas, way to go! If you struggle to be comfortable and confident in your physical body, you are not alone. Things may get even more challenging as you enter your teen years. If you feel uncomfortable and unhappy in the skin and body that you are in, the experience can have a big impact on your daily mood and stress. The good news is, there are many things you can do to shift your relationship with your body. Check out chapter 4 on lots of ideas to get you started. In the meantime, take a minute to reflect on the following questions:

Are there times when you feel uncomfortable in your body or wish you could look like someone else?
What do you imagine you would feel or think about yourself if you looked like that person?

Another thing you can blame for mood challenges is the **developmental stage** (a fancy word for the part of your life you are in) associated with this age. At each part of our life, there is a psychological goal that we ideally meet.

Right now, you are probably facing two big life challenges:

- gaining a sense of confidence and
- developing your identity (who you are and what is important to you).

You begin to see yourself more in relation to others and are trying to find your place among your peers. You may notice that you compare yourself to others a lot, especially in terms of how you are doing in school academically.

As you inch closer to teen years, you gain more independence and begin to know yourself in a deeper way. At this age, **YOU ARE FORMING YOUR OWN BELIEFS AND VALUES**, and these may be different from those of your parents and friends. You think about and practice living by your own rules and goals, are becoming more separated from your parents in what you need and think, and your social relationships feel like everything to you. These are all wonderful, empowering things, but they can also lead to lots of stress, worry, confusion, turmoil, and conflict.

YOUR IDENTITY IS WHO YOU ARE AND WHAT IS IMPORTANT TO YOU.

Take a Minute!

Have you noticed that your opinions, views, and values changed in the last few years? Is there a belief or value (like a social justice issue) that you disagree with one of your friends or parents on?

 ON TOP OF ALL OF THIS, YOU ARE FACING REAL LIFE STRESSORS THAT CAN'T BE IGNORED.

School is full of too many social, academic, and personal pressures to even count! Deadlines, grades, difficult teachers, and friend drama are on the menu daily. No wonder so many people your age experience an overall negative, stressed out mood, more intense feelings of sadness and irritability, and faster, more random changes in both of these areas.

 EVEN RELATIVELY SMALL, COMMON STRESSORS CAN CAUSE A NEGATIVE MOOD OR INTENSE REACTIONS AT YOUR AGE.

Common Stressors

- O   Fighting with your sibling
- O   Being teased at school or at home
- O   Getting a bad grade in a class
- O   Feeling pressured to get good grades
- O   Trying hard at something and not succeeding
- O   Not making the team
- O   Losing in a game or messing up in practice
- O   Being pushed out of your friend group
- O   Looking different than your classmates
- O   Not being picked first
- O   Arguing with your parents
- O   Getting in trouble with a teacher
- O   Getting called on in front of the class and not having the answer

Grab a Pen! ✐

Do you know the events, people, or moments that make you feel the worst? School? At home? Practice? Alone? Write down a few things or people that usually bring your mood down. Now, write down a few ideas that could make your tough moments just a little easier.

If you notice that you are in a worse mood when you aren't getting enough rest, try working on healthy sleep habits (you will learn some in Chapter 9). If you notice that you feel the most irritable while you are doing your homework, try listening to your favorite music while you complete it.

So how can you tell if your mood struggles are typical for your age or something more serious?

ASKING FOR HELP IS THE BRAVEST THING YOU CAN DO!

To tell the difference between typical mood swings or emotional experiences and something more serious, such as depression, consider these three things:

- severity,
- duration, and
- areas of impact.

LET'S TAKE A CLOSER LOOK...

SEVERITY basically means how intense and bad the experience feels and looks. In other words, do you:

- have bigger than usual changes in mood (anger, sadness, and irritability)?
- sleep or eat less or more than usual or isolate yourself from others?
- experiment with drugs, nicotine, or alcohol?
- take more risks that are unusual for you?
- feel more lonely, insecure, or nothing at all?
- often feel hopeless, worthless, or have thoughts of suicide?

The more intense these things are, the more likely it might be that you are struggling with depression or another mental health challenge and not just a passing bad mood. It's ok to feel some of these things very intensely once in a while, but it's concerning if it becomes an ongoing issue and happens a lot.

Also, thoughts about wanting to die, suicide, or self-harm behaviors (cutting, doing drugs, drinking, or other reckless behavior) are serious. If you notice these in yourself or a friend, reach out to an adult for help. Chapter 10 has more information on how to do this.

What about **DURATION**? Are there noticeable changes in the symptoms above that last two weeks or longer without a break? If you are experiencing these moods, feelings, thoughts, and actions daily for a short time, like a few days in a row, that is likely normal. For some, these mood symptoms don't get super intense in severity, but actually last at a low level for a very long period of time (even years). This is called **persistent depressive disorder**, and kids who struggle like this tend to describe noticing that these moods, feelings, and thoughts are always there in the background no matter what they are doing.

In terms of **AREAS OF IMPACT**, how many parts of your life are touched by a negative mood and intense mood swings? The more areas, the more likely there is something more going on than just the middle school emotional experience. If your mood is affecting your social life, your grades and academic life, and your relationships at home, it might be something that you want to look at further and make a plan about.

Take a Minute!

If you think your negative mood might fall into any of those categories (super intense, lasts a very long time, and affects many areas of your life), or if you aren't quite sure where it fits, the best thing you can do is talk to an adult (like a parent, teacher, school counselor, nurse, or pastor) and let them know. That way they can help you dig a little deeper to see what is going on and figure out a plan to get you feeling better. For more tips on how to talk to a friend or an adult in your life, and things that you can do if you are struggling, check out Chapter 10.

Not-So-Fun Fact:

▶ About 20 percent of all teens experience depression before they reach adulthood.

▶ Between 10–15% suffer from symptoms at any one time.

▶ Only 30% of teens with depression are being treated for it.

▶ For more info, check out the Mayo Clinic's YouTube channel and type in teen depression.

Now let's look at Jacob and Casey's stories and think about the mood challenges they are facing.

MEET JACOB. Jacob has a few good friends, enjoys playing soccer, and up until this year did not stress too much about his grades. Lately though, he has

JACOB (he/him)

been struggling in math and science, and no matter what he does he can't seem to get his grades up. The problem is, the ways in which Jacob's parents have tried to help him aren't actually helping, and having them do schoolwork with him seems to cause a lot of arguments.

Over the span of this semester, his mood at home, especially around his parents, has been irritable, sad, and down. He's beginning to feel helpless, which makes him even more mad. Jacob has been closing the door to his room, and spending most of his time at home by himself. Jacob enjoys going to school, because he gets to see his friends, but feels awful when he is in math or science class. He isn't great at soccer, but it doesn't seem to bother him too much. His perspective is "I'm on the team to hang out with my friends, not to be a professional soccer player." Jacob's mood is usually pretty good when he is in his room alone or with his friends, and only really dips down when he is spending time with his parents.

MEET CASEY. Casey has been having a hard time since the start of school. Most days, they feel really down and sad for at least a part of the day. They

CASEY (they/them)

can't remember the last time they felt motivated or happy. Casey has experienced a lot of life stressors. Their parents got divorced when they were 11, they had to move to a new school district after their first year of middle school, and they lost their grandmother to cancer last year.

On the other hand, Casey has also experienced a lot of successes and moments that would make anyone else feel proud, accomplished, and joyful. Just this past year, they got the position of captain of the school's debate team and lead the way to winning a big tournament. After having a tough time finding friends at their new school, they ended up becoming very close with their two current best friends. Casey feels confident, accepted, and comfortable during GSA meetings at school but always feels a nagging sense of hopelessness in the background.

Although they are happy when good things happen, and feel close to their friends, it seems like something is missing. Almost like they are walking around everyday carrying a super heavy backpack that makes every activity feel harder than it should.

Casey's body often feels heavy, and they don't seem to have the energy that their friends do on the weekends. At least once a week, Casey noticed having thoughts like "Things would just be so much easier if I wasn't here or alive," and "Life is too hard, what is the point of even trying?"

PRO TIP

You will be happy to hear that Casey talked with their parents about how they had been feeling. Together as a family, they decided to find a therapist who specialized in treating depression, and Casey is feeling a lot better. Though their life isn't perfect, they feel happy more often, and more in control of their moods.

Common, Typical,

Here are examples of when a mood challenge is common, typical, or cause for concern. If you are feeling any of those red flags, talk to a trusted adult right away.

COMPLETELY COMMON

▶ Having lots of different feelings from moment to moment in a single day

▶ Feelings about something or someone changing, and changing, and then changing again

▶ Having several seemingly opposite or conflicting feelings about something or someone at the very same time (like admiration and anger)

▶ Having a feeling and not being able to identify or name what it is

▶ Having big feelings in the moment and only calming down later

OR a RED FLAG?

NOT UNCOMMON AND TOTALLY TYPICAL

- ▶ Intense temporary fluctuations in mood throughout the day
- ▶ Having a big emotional reaction and taking an action that you regret
- ▶ Getting stuck in a really negative mood for a few hours or days
- ▶ Being in a good mood at school but feeling irritable at home (or vice versa)
- ▶ Saying something you don't mean in the heat of the moment
- ▶ Not feeling fully comfortable in your body
- ▶ Lacking confidence and comparing yourself to your friends

RED FLAG!

- ▶ Feelings so intense that you have the urge to harm yourself (or actually harm yourself)
- ▶ Thinking about suicide
- ▶ Feeling down most of the day for more than a few weeks
- ▶ Feeling a little bit down all of the time for as long as you can remember

LET'S CHANGE GEARS. Does reading about all of the stressors that you face at your age make you feel overwhelmed? It's easy to focus on the negative, but you already know that thinking about only the negatives can leave you stuck in a bad mood.

Let's practice **INTENTIONALLY NOTICING** the positive and take a look at some of the wonderful things that can happen at your age.

MIDDLE SCHOOL IS... GREAT! Check out some common things that kids your age say on the next page that create a positive joyful mood and make middle school great!

FOCUSING ON THE POSITIVE AND TAKING POSITIVE ACTIONS CAN MAKE A HUGE DIFFERENCE IN YOUR MOOD OVER TIME.

A Call to Action:

Positive affirmations are one way to help your mind focus on the good things in your life. I love "I am enough," and "I can do hard things." Think of a few more statements that feel right for you and repeat them to yourself each day.

What's "great" about Middle School?

- ☐ Seeing your friends every day at school
- ☐ Walking to school with friends or on your own
- ☐ Figuring out your strengths and weaknesses
- ☐ Choosing what movies you watch
- ☐ Spending time with someone you care about
- ☐ Having freedom to do the things you enjoy
- ☐ Being proud of yourself for something you achieved or noticed in yourself
- ☐ Winning a game or feeling a lot of team spirit even if you lose
- ☐ Finishing the semester
- ☐ Summer
- ☐ Getting to know yourself and finding your own values
- ☐ Developing your own opinions

Grab a Pen!

Do you know what helps you feel joy & accomplishment? Grab a notebook and write down some of the things that you know tend to put you in a positive mood. What are you actually liking about middle school? If your brain is saying "nothing," see if you can dig a little deeper and find something, even something small. What is usually the happiest moment of your week? Make a plan to do at least one thing that might bring you joy or make you feel accomplished every day.

Take-Away!

THE MORE YOU KNOW, THE MORE YOU CAN SHIFT YOUR PERSPECTIVE! Right now, you are facing some obstacles in terms of maintaining a balanced, positive mood, as well as consistently managing intense emotions. There are lots of factors involved here:

 biology (your feeling brain is developing faster than your thinking brain, and your hormones are shifting)

 social and emotional development (adjusting to a changing body, navigating different social relationships, finding your independence, and finding your own voice, values, beliefs, and goals)

⭐ life stressors (so much academic, family, and social pressure!)

It's not always easy to tease apart what is "typical" given these challenges, and what is concerning enough that you should ask for help from an adult. Psychologists have three major rules that can help you get clarity about your experience, including noticing how long lasting your negative mood and emotional ups and downs are, how intense they feel, and how many areas of your life feel negative and unpredictable.

But there are a lot of wonderful things that happen at your age too, and focusing on them can help you shift your perspective. The more you know about yourself and your mood, the more you can take charge and make small changes that can have a big impact on your well-being.

Chapter 3

It's All in Your Brain!

*T*here is a lot we still have to learn, but here is what we do know: there are aspects of brain structure and activity that are critically involved in creating our mood.

You might be thinking, "Why am I reading about about neuroscience?" or "I didn't sign up for bio class!" But stay with me! The information will be so helpful as you learn to shift your mood and outlook. I'll keep it short and sweet with a little fun mixed in. When you can understand what's going on in your brain, it allows you to understand yourself better, to get some distance from your emotions, and helps you see things from a more helpful perspective.

In this chapter, I'll discuss the relationship between your thinking brain and your feeling brain, as well as how your brain chemicals and hormones work together to create your emotions and mood. Most importantly, a negative mood, big feelings that seem impossible to control, and trouble "snapping out of it" will make a whole lot more sense, giving you the power to understand yourself on a deeper level and begin to feel better.

WHEN WE CAN UNDERSTAND OUR BRAIN, WE CAN UNDERSTAND OURSELVES!

BRAIN STRUCTURE

In terms of brain structure, each part of our brain has a role to play and a job to do. The two areas most associated with mood and self-regulation are the limbic system and the prefrontal cortex. Together, these parts of the brain communicate and form what scientists have called the **emotion circuit** of the brain.

Our limbic system is a set of structures, the most well-known of which are the **amygdala** and **hippocampus**, that are responsible for managing our response to emotional events and reinforcing our behavior. The limbic system is probably most famous for the **fight-flight-freeze response**, which was basically designed to keep us alive and save our life in moments of extreme danger.

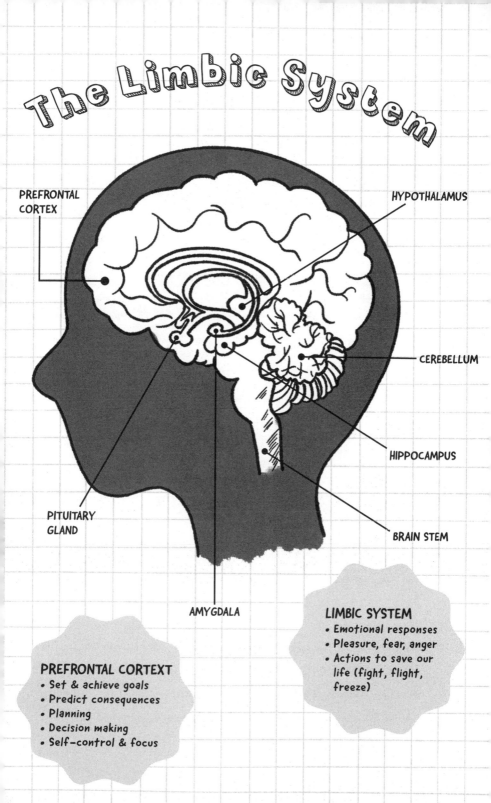

The Limbic System

PREFRONTAL CORTEX

HYPOTHALAMUS

CEREBELLUM

HIPPOCAMPUS

PITUITARY GLAND

BRAIN STEM

AMYGDALA

PREFRONTAL CORTEXT
- Set & achieve goals
- Predict consequences
- Planning
- Decision making
- Self-control & focus

LIMBIC SYSTEM
- Emotional responses
- Pleasure, fear, anger
- Actions to save our life (fight, flight, freeze)

Fun Fact:

In those who have more trouble self-regulating, and those prone to depression, these brain regions show abnormalities in their size, cerebral blood flow, and glucose metabolism, as well as differences in activity levels in response to environmental triggers. All of this to say, what you're feeling is being reflected in how your brain is working, and vice versa!

PRO TIP

When most people think of the fight-flight-freeze response, very intense situations come to mind, like coming face-to-face with a bear! But this response can happen all the time in your daily life, like when you can't think of anything to say to your crush or when you argue with your sibling. So while this physiological response is critical to saving our life in moments of true danger, it works like a false alarm sometimes in our daily lives. Sort of like outdated software, it worked well when we were struggling to survive each day, but now it just jams things up and keeps us stuck.

The prefrontal cortex is responsible for our ability to control and respond to emotional experiences and regulate our mood.

THE PREFRONTAL CORTEX IS THE "THINKING" PART OF YOUR BRAIN AND THE LIMBIC SYSTEM IS THE "FEELING" PART OF YOUR BRAIN.

It helps to imagine the prefrontal cortex as your wisest, smartest, most level-headed friend who always seems to do the "right" or "responsible" thing. Your parents probably love this friend. Maybe this friend is actually you?

Now, think of the limbic system as your most impulsive, loud, intense, charismatic friend, who somehow always ends up in trouble. When something happens that evokes a strong emotional reaction, like getting a bad grade or being left out of a friend group, the prefrontal cortex usually tries to talk some sense into the limbic system, to slow things down, think things through, and make a smart choice. To keep things simple throughout the rest of this book, I'll continue to refer to the prefrontal cortex as the thinking brain, and the limbic system as the feeling brain.

THINK OF THE AMYGDALA, HIPPOCAMPUS, AND PREFRONTAL CORTEX AS BEST FRIENDS THAT ALWAYS WORK TOGETHER TO FULFILL THEIR NUMBER ONE JOB—CREATE YOUR EMOTIONAL WORLD.

Fun Fact:

The hippocampus, which is involved in learning and memory, context-dependent emotional responses, and calming down the HPA axis (our body's response system to stress), is one of the most neuroplastic (changeable) parts of the brain. New neurons in it continue to grow and mature throughout our entire lives. Yes! You CAN teach an old dog new tricks!

BACK STORY: Hippocampus, who remembers everything bad that has ever happened (it is responsible for storing emotional memories), is freaking out because it learns that there is a pop quiz in English. The last time this happened, both Hippocampus and Amygdala (the most emotional of this group of friends) burst into tears after getting their grades back. Hippocampus runs out of the classroom and starts racing down the hallway. All it wants to do is hide in the bathroom.

Amygdala, seeing all of this happen, overhears a few classmates making fun of Hippocampus for being so afraid. Amygdala wants to run too, but instead starts to boil with anger and immediately has the urge to run over to the person making fun of Hippocampus. If left to its own devices, Amygdala might start screaming, flailing its arms, maybe even pushing and throwing that person to the floor.

Prefrontal Cortex is standing by and notices the wider context—it sees the teacher looking directly at them, and is able to talk Amygdala down and pull it back from doing something they would all get in trouble for. Prefrontal Cortex reminds Amygdala that this fight will not be worth the trouble. When this friend group, or emotional circuit, is functioning and working together well, Prefrontal Cortex is able to talk to its friends when stressful things happen, and they figure out a wise action together. When the friend group isn't getting along well or communicating quickly, Amygdala and Hippocampus end up feeling mad, sad, and helpless, and make decisions that are not very wise.

Fun Fact:

Though the amygdala and hippocampus are the most extensively studied and understood, there are many other structures that are part of the limbic system, including: limbic cortex (containing the cingulate gyrus and parahippocampal gyrus), the hippocampal formation (housing the dentate gyrus, hippocampus, and subicular complex), the septal area, and the hypothalamus. Now say those ten times quickly and back-to-back!

Take a Minute!

Think about a time where your feeling brain was out of control and could have used some more help from the thinking brain. Have you ever rushed to a decision you later regretted? Have you ever frozen in place instead of taking an action you knew would make you feel better (like inviting a friend to hang out)?

BRAIN ACTIVITY

In terms of brain activity, research has shown that a long lasting bad mood like what we see in people with depression is associated with an imbalance among certain **neurotransmitters** (neurochemicals that help our brain cells communicate with each other) and **hormones** (chemical messengers through which the brain communicates with the rest of our body via the bloodstream). A balance between our brain chemicals and our hormones is extremely important when it comes to feeling well emotionally.

PRO TIP

Did you know that just by putting your hands on your heart (or other area of the body) you send a signal to your body's calm-down circuit?

IN TERMS OF NEUROTRANSMITTERS. Though it's more complicated than what can be described in one chapter, the brain communicates with itself by sending chemicals (neuro-transmitters) from one neuron, or nerve, to another. This messaging plays a role in how we feel. In general, there are two big categories of neurotransmitters—ones that increase brain activity (**excitatory**) and ones that calm the brain (**inhibitory**). Some of the most widely studied neurotransmitters when it comes to mood are serotonin, dopamine, glutamate, and norepinephrine. Let's take a look at what each one of these neurochemicals does!

SEROTONIN

helps us feel focused, emotionally stable, happy, and calm. The receptors for serotonin are often targeted by antidepressant medications because of their strong impact on mood and depressive symptoms.

DOPAMINE

controls many of our brain's functions, including our mood, behavior, emotions, sleep, memory, and concentration. It helps motivate us to do things that make us feel good.

GLUTAMATE

has been linked to depression and mood problems. An imbalance in glutamate levels is associated with mood swings, and certain mental health difficulties including mood disorders and schizophrenia.

NOREPINEPHRINE

helps regulate mood, emotions, and our ability to concentrate. It has been linked to depression, anxiety, post-traumatic stress disorder, substance use, and is involved in our body's fight-flight-freeze response.

Fun Fact:

Most of our serotonin is stored in our intestine, not in our brain! Scientists believe it may play a role in our digestive functioning.

Why does an imbalance among our neurotransmitters occur? There are many things that can contribute:

- long periods of stress
- poor nutrition
- genetic factors (thanks, parents!)
- toxic substances or drugs, including caffeine, alcohol, and nicotine
- hormone changes

IN TERMS OF HORMONES. The second category of brain activity associated with mood lies with hormones. There is a close relationship between neurotransmitters and hormones—some neurotransmitters, such as norepinephrine, are also hormones, and others have a direct effect on how hormones are released in the body.

Hormones are usually made by specialist cells in the endocrine gland and released into the body, where they communicate between organs and the rest of the body or between distant parts of the body. The hormones most widely associated with our mood and emotional functioning, along with norepinephrine, are adrenaline and cortisol—their balance affects the way our mood, emotions, and stress are triggered.

LET'S LOOK AT SOME MORE SPECIFICS.

HORMONES

NOREPINEPHRINE

is both a hormone and a neurotransmitter and is
made by the adrenal glands to help us
regulate our body's response to stress.

- High levels = happiness
- Low levels = panic, low energy,
  low focus, depression, ADHD

CORTISOL is often called

the "stress" hormone and is also made in the
adrenal glands and helps control the body's
response to stress.

- Too high = anxiety and depression
- Too low = weakness, fatigue, and low blood
  pressure

ADRENALINE

is a hormone also made by the adrenal glands and is a crucial part of our fight-flight-freeze response. When we are in a stressful situation, adrenaline is quickly released into the bloodstream to activate our body to save our life.

- Balanced = saves our life (fight-flight-freeze response active)
- Unbalanced = irritability, restlessness, anxiety, panic

 TO LEARN MORE ABOUT HORMONES AND HOW THEY WORK, GO TO:
https://www.yourhormones.info/hormones/

Why are you learning about all of these brain processes, neurotransmitters, and hormones? When you know more about what is going on in your brain, it is easier to shift your perspective, feel more in control, and understand yourself better. The more you understand, the more power you have.

THE BAD NEWS: we obviously do not have full control over the processes in the brain. All of this information can make you feel helpless and hopeless about managing your feelings. If these things go on in the brain, without you even realizing it, how can you get any control?

THE GOOD NEWS: there are things you can do to have an impact on your brain functioning and activity. The power you have to change your brain lies in **neuroplasticity**. This is your brain's ability to change and grow, and it is truly amazing.

Scientists have discovered that we can actually regrow brain cells and change the structure and function of our brain by changing how we think, what we believe, and taking different actions. That's right: **YOU CAN USE YOUR MIND TO CHANGE YOUR BRAIN.** In particular, by changing your thoughts, beliefs, mindset, and actions, you can strengthen the ability of your thinking brain to calm down and communicate with your feeling brain.

WE CAN CHANGE OUR BRAIN BY CHANGING WHAT WE THINK, BELIEVE, AND HOW WE ACT.

All of the strategies you'll master by reading this book and practicing these skills are related to cognitive-behavioral therapy. Your mind, body, and behavior are all connected. It's sort of like you are strengthening the powers of your thinking brain and giving it more time to talk some sense into your feeling brain. And then that affects how you act and react. Am I winning you over with the whole **"BRAINS ARE SO COOL"** idea yet?

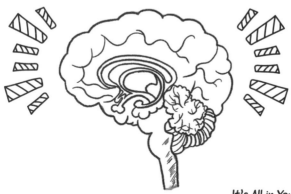

Along with working on changing our thinking, beliefs, and actions, these daily activities have been shown to change our brain activity and in turn our mood:

- feeding our bodies nutritious food
- exercising
- limiting our daily stress levels
- getting enough sleep, meditating
- listening to music
- getting outside in sunlight
- even eating chocolate!

You will learn more about these strategies later in this book, and you can pick and choose which ones to add to your life.

PRO TIP

Researchers have found that engaging in cognitive-behavioral therapy (which focuses on learning more helpful ways of thinking, shifting one's beliefs, and engaging in activating behaviors) can lead to meaningful changes in the brain areas involved in mood and self-regulation, including the amygdala-hippocampal complex and the prefrontal cortex.

Take-Away!

The way our brain works is very complex, and we have a long way to go before we can fully understand it. But based on what we know so far, challenges with our mood, poor emotion processing, and impulsive responding to emotional experiences happen when there is an imbalance among the structures and activity of certain parts of the brain. The areas of the brain most strongly connected to our mood are the limbic system and the prefrontal cortex, both of which are thought to make up the emotional circuit of the brain.

We can think of our prefrontal cortex as our thinking brain and our limbic system as our feeling brain. Our mood and self-regulation are in trouble when there is decreased activity in the thinking brain, which helps regulate and calm the feeling brain, and when there is increased activity in the feeling brain.

Neurotransmitters and hormones are also involved in our mood. Neurotransmitters are chemicals that allow the brain to communicate with itself. Horomones are messengers that help our brain communicate with and activate our body. Some noteworthy neurotransmitters and hormones to remember for mood regulation include: serotonin, dopamine, glutamate, norepinephrine, adrenaline, and coristol. They all communicate with the body.

The great news is, scientists are learning that changing the way we think, shifting our beliefs, and taking new and different actions can help our thinking brain more effectively communicate with and calm down our feeling brain.

This information is important to think about as you read this book because it applies directly to you! During this time in your life, your thinking brain is significantly lagging behind your feeling brain in terms of development and activity. When you are armed with information, it's much easier to shift your perspective about your own mood and emotional responses, and to ultimately feel better on a daily basis.

chapter 4

Move Your Mood!

*E*ver notice your mood in your body? Maybe you're grumpy and your shoulders are tight. Maybe you're happy and you feel light and bright! Your body is telling you something, and information is POWER.

You can learn how to move your body and shift your body's energy in ways that can improve your mood and confidence. There are a ton of activities that almost everyone can add to their life—whether you love moving, hate moving, have athletic talent or not, and no matter what your abilities are. The importance of movement and connecting with your body can't be overstated.

You're probably thinking, "Wait. I have heard a million times that I should exercise. No way. I don't like it, don't feel good when I do it, and it just makes me feel worse when I try."

Well, you're not alone— but try to give this chapter a chance. It could just be the missing link to more joy and well-being. You can **TAKE CHARGE** of your body and mood by creating a personalized relationship with physical movement. It doesn't have to be structured "workouts" or sports if that's not what you are into! You can do this—and more importantly, you can do this **YOUR WAY,** while focusing on feeling strong, confident, and grateful for how your body is able to move no matter what your current fitness level, ability, or body size is.

THE KEY IS TO HAVE GRATITUDE AND RESPECT FOR WHAT YOUR BODY CAN DO, INSTEAD OF FOCUSING ON ALL THE THINGS IT CAN'T.

A Call to Action:

If you could use a boost in gratitude for your body and what it can do, try a loving-kindness meditation for your body before you start any of the body movements or exercises I discuss in this chapter. Loving-kindness mediations send love, kindness, and compassion by directing positive thoughts toward ourselves or others. It's also been shown to reduce anxiety, increase feelings of hope, and increase feelings of self-love. You can use some of the apps in our resources section to help guide you through one.

CREATING A HEALTHY RELATIONSHIP WITH YOUR BODY AND WITH MOVEMENT IS ABOUT HOW POWERFUL AND CONFIDENT YOU FEEL ON THE INSIDE. Frustration, helplessness, hopelessness, shame, irritability, and anger, when experienced non-stop or often, seriously affect your mood and lead to chronic stress inside your body. And that can shift your body's hormone balance, depleting the very brain chemicals that you need in order to feel good and keep your immune system running well.

That's right—your mood can even affect your health!

Your mood has a huge impact on how your body looks on the outside—and how other people see you. You probably recognize that people use body language intentionally to express themselves, their thoughts, and their emotions: for example, clapping to offer praise to someone or smiling to express joy. What you might not realize is that we also move our bodies based on how we feel without even realizing it. The **TONE OF YOUR VOICE, PHYSICAL POSTURE, BODY POSITION RELATIVE TO OTHERS, AND FACIAL EXPRESSIONS** all show the mood you are in, and also have the power to make others feel a certain way towards you.

Importantly, the way your body feels, the way you carry yourself physically, and how others respond to you, can have a major impact on your mood. This is how the negative mood cycle continues.

 How does my body and the way I move affect my mood?

When your body feels heavy or stuck, and your posture is slouched and closed off, you are creating negative energy that can lead to and keep a negative mood going.

But when you are in a positive mood, your posture tends to be open, you smile more, hold your head up high, and look at others with warmth. That positive energy allows you to stay in a good mood.

When your body is slow, down, and tense, it is hard to take HELPFUL actions. It might be hard to go outside, reach out to a friend, or start on homework. Everything takes more effort!

People might think you want to be alone or that you're unfriendly. They are less likely to want to talk to you or get to know you. Even your friends might act more distant!

When your mood stays stuck, you feel more alone, lonely, and down. And the cycle continues.

When your body feels energized, open, tall, and relaxed, you have more energy and easily take actions to engage in things you love doing!

When you are actively doing things that bring you joy or a sense of accomplishment, your mood tends to be more positive. You are perceived as warm and friendly, making it easier for others to connect with you. You're buzzing with positive energy!

When you are more connected with others and feel supported and noticed,

the cycle continues to feed your positive mood.

 How can I use my body to change my mood and feel better?

Now for the good stuff. To help you master your mood and well-being, let's focus on **activation** and **self-soothing strategies**. Here I'll talk about how to move your body in precise and easy-to-learn ways that will seriously improve your mood.

ACTIVATION!

Activation basically means getting your body moving. Like striking a match to light a fire! It's doing actions to help you tap into your energy reserves, warm up your body, and really get your adrenaline pumping, making it easier to get through your day and flow into a positive mood.

Three excellent ways to activate the body are **JUMP STARTS, ENERGIZING YOGA POSES**, and, for when you have a bit more time, good ol' **PHYSICAL WORKOUTS**.

Physical movement of any kind is so important to your well-being and mood for so many reasons. Movement promotes changes in the brain, including growth of new neurons (remember neuroplasticity?), reduced inflammation, and new activity patterns that create a sense of calm. Also, physical exercise signals the brain to release **endorphins** (powerful chemicals in our brain that make us feel good and make us feel happy). As you read and think about what works for you, choose movements that are available to your body on any given day or time. Whatever works for you is perfect! **PERIOD.**

Shame, embarrassment, and self-criticism have no home here.

Pay attention to how your body feels going through these movements. I've tried to include movements that can easily be modified for people with a wide range of movement abilities, but if a movement is not available to your body, **THAT IS OK!** Take this as data about what works and what doesn't.

FIND A WAY TO MOVE THAT MOVES YOU!

If you only have a couple minutes, try short bursts of intense movement: **JUMP STARTS.** It sounds silly, but trust me, this can be very helpful to get your day going strong.

Each 1 or 2 minute burst really packs a big punch. Can't use the "I don't have time" excuse—they only last a couple minutes! There is no right or wrong way here—you can choose one of these movements to do first thing every morning after getting out of bed. The goal is to get your heart rate up!

Jump Starts include:

- Jumping jacks
- Jogging as quickly as you can in place
- Running up and down the stairs
- Air squats

A Call to Action:

If you choose to do any of the body movements I describe in this chapter, make note of which ones you like and don't like. You can even find a local group of people who enjoy the same activities and you can join them!

If you only have 5 or 10 minutes, you could try **ENERGIZING YOGA POSES**. Think of these poses as postures that help you access your best, most energetic, positive, and confident self. All you have to do is hold these poses for 30 to 60 seconds or for as long as it feels right for your body. Then repeat the pose a couple times for a total of 5 to 10 minutes.

Mountain Pose

Stand with your feet well balanced and grounded on the floor. Gently pull your bellybutton inward and tighten your belly. At the same time, open your chest and stand as tall as you can. Imagine your body long and tall, like you are reaching the top of your head up towards the sky as you lengthen your spine. Make sure to keep gently pulling your belly inwards while you lengthen. For extra energy, raise your arms straight overhead while taking a big inhale with your palms facing one another, and hold for a few breaths. Focus on opening your chest and heart, standing tall, belly in, and grounding your feet into the floor.

Down Dog Into Up Dog

Get into plank position, lift your hips up towards the sky, lengthening the back of your legs and pressing your heels to the floor (it's ok if they don't touch). Press your hands into the floor as you keep lifting your hips back to feel your spine and legs lengthen. Gently shift back to plank pose, and on your inhale lower your hips/knees so that they almost touch the floor, and lift your chest up, pressing your hands into the floor. Breathe deeply and roll your shoulders back to open your chest and heart area. You can lower your knees all the way to the floor if the knees-up position is not available to you. Alternate slowly back and forth between the poses for as long as it feels good.

Tree Pose

Standing tall with both feet on the ground, bend your right knee and place your right foot either against your left calf or high on your left inner thigh. Just don't put it against your left knee (this is bad for your knee joint!). You may keep your hands on your hips or bring them into prayer position (palms together in front of you). Press your right foot and left inner thigh into each other as your left foot continues to ground through the floor. Overachievers—raise your arms up to get tall, open your chest while still pulling the belly inward (try not to allow your front ribs to open forward too much). Breathe and enjoy the firm, grounded, positive energy before switching sides.

PRO TIP

If you want to up the intensity of these poses and are needing to feel even more positive energy, here are some of our favorite sayings to use: Repeat these to yourself quietly, loudly, or in your mind as you breathe.

Inhale energy, exhale fatigue

Breathe in confidence, exhale doubt

Inhale power, exhale fear

With each breath, positive in, negative out

Inhale positive vibes, and exhale anything that is not helping me

The mood-boosting benefits of regular movement and **PHYSICAL EXERCISE** are endless:

- increased energy,
- better sleep,
- decreased stress,
- improved confidence,
- improved memory,
- increased feelings of relaxation, and
- decreased levels of pain

….just to name a few. Regular exercise can also have a major impact on symptoms of depression, anxiety, chronic pain, and ADHD. The World Health Organization suggest that teenagers:

- spend 60 minutes per day in moderate-to-vigorous intensity movement, and
- three days a week, include some high intensity aerobic or strength training activities.

You could fill your 60 minutes of daily exercise with all sorts of movement: walking, running, biking, any sport, yoga, dance, Pilates, cycling, strength training with or without weights, rowing, paddle boarding, and outrunning zombies, just to name a few. So add up your minutes! You might be doing more than 60 minutes just moving around school or seeing your friends in your neighborhood in-between your more typical exercise.

PRO TIP

Don't overthink the amount of time you need to spend moving or the type of activity. If the guidelines feel like too much, you're not alone, and you can take it step by step. Even if you don't meet the WHO guidelines, **ANY AMOUNT OF PHYSICAL ACTIVITY IS BETTER THAN NONE.** You'll still get some great mood benefits. The key to incorporating physical movement in your daily life is finding something that you enjoy and being consistent.

EVERYONE CAN FIND GRATITUDE FOR THEIR BODY. TRAIN YOUR BRAIN TO SPOT ALL THE THINGS THAT YOU CAN DO INSTEAD OF ONLY NOTICING THE THINGS YOU CAN'T.

SELF-SOOTHING ACTIVITIES

SELF-SOOTHING is the second major category of body strategies that are helpful in managing our mood. Think of activation as waking up and opening the body, and self-soothing as calming down and relaxing the body. Two very different effects on the body, and both are just as important for our mood. The ability to self-soothe when we are feeling down, sad, angry, or overwhelmed is critical to a balanced mood, not to mention a positive relationship with ourselves. The three skills you'll learn and practice while reading this section are calm breathing, relaxing yoga poses, and soothing touch.

YOU PROBABLY DON'T REMEMBER, BUT WHEN YOU WERE AN INFANT YOU MIGHT HAVE SUCKED ON YOUR THUMB OR HUGGED A BLANKET. THOSE ARE SELF-SOOTHING STRATEGIES, TOO.

There are many ways to practice **CALM BREATHING**— also called diaphragmatic breathing, deep breathing, or belly breathing. There is no one way to do it, but there are ways to make it work more effectively for you.

Some people prefer to stretch out their inhale and exhale for as long as possible, some people like to add a short hold of their breath at the top of their inhale before exhaling, and others prefer to count to a specific number of seconds per inhale and exhale.

Either way, make sure that you are inhaling all the way down into your belly, letting your whole midsection expand on all sides like you have a balloon in your stomach. The most effective method for you will be the one that feels easiest when you try it, and the one you **ENJOY** the most. If you ever are feeling lightheaded or too short of breath, try slowing the pace, changing the pattern, or skipping the "holding" part. You'll figure out what's most comfortable for you. Pretty simple, right?

Let's practice one of these to see how you do. If it turns out you love calm breathing, try to do it at least once per day. Any time works, but many people like to practice early in the morning to start the day and late in the evening to calm down before sleep.

 How do you think the calm breathing will help? Take note of how you are feeling before, during, and after.

Box Breathing

Practice the following breathing pattern for 10 minutes if you have time, or for 10 breaths in a pinch. Inhale for four slow seconds. Then, hold your breath at the top of the inhale for four slow seconds. Slowly exhale for four slow seconds. Then, hold your breath at the end of the exhale for four slow seconds.

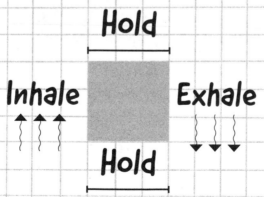

Repeat!

Think of **RELAXING YOGA POSES** as the fastest way to turn down the volume on the intensity of a negative emotion and mood. These poses are often done towards the end of yoga classes to turn on the body's calming system. These poses feel so amazing and soothing. You can use them anytime you get stuck in a negative mood or notice a negative emotion getting more intense, but the best way to practice is by incorporating them into your daily routine for a few minutes each day. This way you improve your skills bit by bit, so that you can be ready for moments that are more challenging.

Rag Doll

Stand with your hands on your hips, exhale, and gently bend your knees slightly as you bend at the waist and allow your upper body to drape over your legs. For extra soothing, sway your upper body gently from side to side while holding your arms folded at the elbow, or shake your head yes and no.

Extended Puppy Pose

Get into a position on the floor on your hands and knees,
walk your hands forward to lengthen the spine and feel
a deep stretch in your upper back and shoulders. Keep
shifting your hips up towards the sky and open your
heart towards the floor. Deeply breathe to fill your lungs,
slowly exhale any energy or thought that isn't serving you.

Child's Pose

Kneel on the floor, touch your big toes together, and sit
back on your heels with your knees separated as wide
as your hips. Lay your torso down between your thighs.
Focus on inching the hands forward and allowing your
hips to lengthen and sink back.

Soothing Touch

Connecting your hands to specific parts of your body can be incredibly soothing and can be added to calm breathing and relaxing yoga poses to intensify their power.

If it sounds like I am being dramatic, trust me, the power of touch really can be that intense. The moment you bring your hands to your heart or belly (or both), your brain sends a signal to your body's calming system to turn on. Another way of saying this is that physical touch can instantly relax your body.

Take a Minute!

Place one hand on your belly, and one hand on your heart. Close your eyes and allow yourself to breathe naturally for a few moments. Powerful, right?

YOU HOLD THE POWER TO INSTANTLY RELAX YOUR BODY JUST BY CONNECTING WITH IT BY TOUCH.

Take a Minute!

Sit or stand as tall as you can, relax your shoulders, look straight ahead, and take a few deep breaths. Were you slouching before? What did you notice as you shifted your posture? Check in on your body a few times per day, notice your posture, and see if you can change your body to instantly shift your emotional state.

A Call to Action:

Choose one of each of these strategies to focus on and practice once daily. Pick one activating exercise (energizing yoga pose, short burst of movement, or 45 minutes of a workout), and one self-soothing exercise (relaxing yoga pose, calm breathing, or soothing touch) that worked for you, and make them a habit!

Take-Away!

Your body plays an important role in your mood. When your body is light and energetic, it is easier to take positive actions, and you seem approachable and friendly to others. When your mood is down, you can use strategies to shift your body in a way that makes it easier to take positive actions, makes it more likely that you get support from others, and makes you feel more positive and confident. You can shift how you feel and how others see you just by changing your posture. People who hold their bodies in an upright, tall, open stance, make good eye contact, and smile look more confident and friendly.

What's more, if you shift your posture slightly, you may notice feeling more relaxed and powerful. There are many things you can do to take charge of your body and shift your mood, including:

 shifting your posture: upright, tall, open chest, relaxed shoulders, and smiling

★ activation strategies: energizing yoga poses, jump starts, and more regular workouts

★ self-soothing strategies: relaxing yoga poses, calm breathing, soothing touch

Please know that, when it comes to creating a healthy relationship with physical movement, there is something for everyone. The key is to find something that YOU enjoy doing, that makes you feel good on the inside.

A note on body image: Human bodies come in all sorts of shapes, sizes, heights, and weights. Creating a healthy relationship with your body and with movement is not about the way it looks on the outside, it is about how **POWERFUL** and **CONFIDENT** you feel on the inside.

Chapter 5

Mood, Emotions, and Keeping It All Together... 😁

ou've already learned that an **EMOTION** is an in-the-moment experience that lasts for a short time. When we feel an uncomfortable emotion, we can use **SELF-REGULATION** to find balance, discover what is important to us, and take actions that help us get out of a negative mood or stay firmly in a positive mood. On the other hand, if we get stuck in a negative emotion or try to avoid it altogether, we tend to take actions that are unhelpful or miss out on opportunities to make choices that would help make us feel better.

SELF-REGULATION IS A POWERFUL SET OF SKILLS THAT HELP YOU FEEL BALANCED, CALM, AND STABLE THROUGHOUT THE UPS AND DOWNS OF LIFE.

With **INTENTIONAL PRACTICE**, you have the power to manage your emotions in healthy ways, so you can stay in a positive mood more often or get out of a negative mood when you get stuck. With strong self-regulation, you can experience, notice, evaluate, and shift your actions in a way that serves you instead of harming you. One important way to manage your emotions is called **mindfulness**. Mindfulness involves noticing, naming, and accepting your emotions without judgment, criticism, or attempts to change them.

As you practice these strategies, your ability to self-regulate will improve, and you will be much more able to maintain a balanced mood and deal with life's ups and downs without crumbling. The bottom line is, if you can self-regulate and manage your emotions, you will breeze through things that would bring most people down. By the end of this chapter, I hope you will feel much more confident about your ability to handle anything life throws your way.

PRO TIP

There are times when emotions can become incredibly confusing and very intense. During these moments when emotions feel totally out of our control, it is hard to self-regulate, and you may take impulsive actions that you later regret, leaving you stuck in a deep negative mood. This is called emotional dysregulation or FLOODING. You'll learn more about how to deal with these very uncomfortable emotional experiences, as well as how to get your power back, in Chapter 10.

MOOD AND EMOTIONS

There are so many different emotions available to us that I can't possibly name them all in one chapter, but in general, some emotions are enjoyable, such as happiness, joy, excitement, pride, and love, while other emotions can feel very uncomfortable, like sadness, anger, fear, disgust, embarrassment, guilt, and shame.

Along with your body sensations and your thoughts, your emotions impact the actions that you take or don't take, and thus impact your mood. Enjoyable emotions help you stay in a positive mood, and uncomfortable emotions, when not managed in healthy ways, can really throw your mood off. There are a few ways in which uncomfortable emotions feed into a feedback cycle including:

1. Getting fully stuck in an emotion leads to a negative mindset that makes it hard to take actions that could improve mood.

2. If you avoid or ignore an uncomfortable emotion, you miss out on important information about yourself. Emotions help you discover what is important to you, understand what you want and need, set boundaries, and make good choices.

When you make decisions that are based on your values, you'll have a better chance of staying in a positive mood cycle or getting out of a negative one.

3. If you don't yet have strong skills in managing your emotions, you may jump into a negative mood so intensely that it totally overwhelms you. This makes you more likely to make impulsive choices that you may later regret, creating more self-criticism and blame, and pushing you further into that negative mood cycle.

What does self-regulation look like in **real** life?

Maria does not get invited to a party thrown by the popular kids at her school and only finds out when she sees them post a photo on Instagram. Maria immediately feels a ton of emotions she can't untangle: anger, shame, embarrassment, and sadness. She pretends like nothing is wrong even though her parents and best friend (Christina, who also did not get invited) have asked her if she's ok. Maria feels so down that, instead of replying to Christina and making different plans, she stays home all weekend. Maria's mood stays negative throughout the following week, and each time she thinks about the party, she feels mad all over again.

Casey has the exact same experience. No invite to the party. When they see the post, they notice they are extremely angry and feel the urge to throw their phone. They take a deep breath and try to observe their emotions while letting themselves feel them. They are surprised that in addition to anger, they feel sad and lonely. They don't feel like talking to anyone, but they also know that the feeling of loneliness may be giving them information about a way out. When Christina sends a text about plans for the weekend, Casey takes a breath and replies, knowing that if they feel closer to Christina, they will feel less lonely. Casey still feels some anger and sadness, but it feels a bit more manageable. They also notice feelings of connection and relief that they can rely on Christina (actually several friends!).

At one point, Casey decides to tell Christina about the party they missed out on. Christina makes a joke about the person throwing the party that makes Casey laugh so hard that they almost forget how upset they were. By the end of the weekend, thanks to spending time with Christina and doing things they enjoy, Casey feels confident walking into school and is able to focus on their schoolwork and soccer practice.

Take a Minute!

Have you ever been in Casey or Maria's position? Can you think of an example of your own (or a friend's) where you weren't able to self-regulate in the face of difficult emotions? What do you wish you had done differently? What about a moment where you (or a friend) faced something intensely stressful and managed it successfully?

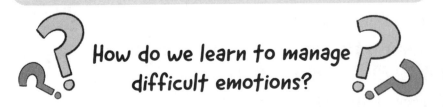

How do we learn to manage difficult emotions?

Many people think that negative or difficult emotions are "bad," and that they should try to avoid or run from them. You may have even heard someone say: "I don't have feelings. I don't get mad." The truth is, we all have lots of different emotions inside of us at any given time.

ALL EMOTIONS ARE IMPORTANT SOURCES OF INFORMATION.

Emotions give us data, which helps us know ourselves in a deeper way and make small and big decisions that impact our mood. So how do you maximize the information you get from your emotions without getting stuck or taking an impulsive or unhelpful action? Practice mindfulness!

There are three steps to learning mindfulness when it comes to tough emotions:

Notice » Name » Accept

STEP 1: **NOTICE**

Noticing when you have an uncomfortable emotion is the first step to mastering your emotional experience. This may sound easy and obvious, but it's much harder than you might think. Why? When you are experiencing an intense emotion, the part of your brain that gets super activated is your feeling brain. When this part of the emotion circuit gets turned up, our thinking brain gets turned down and we're less likely to make good decisions.

WHAT DOES THIS MEAN?

The very moment when our emotions are super intense is the very moment when we don't have easy access to our wisest ways of thinking and acting. This is where noticing and naming come in—they help our thinking brain turn up the volume.

WHEN WE FEEL AN INTENSE EMOTION, OUR FEELING BRAIN IS TURNED UP, AND OUR THINKING BRAIN IS TURNED DOWN.

In order to start the process of helping the thinking brain turn on more, we must first notice that we are experiencing an emotion. Speed is important here—we have the best chance at activating our wisest mind when we notice an emotion at the beginning, before it becomes really intense. Once a negative emotion peaks, it is much more difficult to get in balance. This is because our feeling brain is basically on fire and our thinking brain stands no chance.

Sometimes, you might be really good at noticing that you are experiencing an emotion. You may be better at noticing certain emotions than others, and there may be times where you don't realize you are even feeling an emotion after it has passed. To improve your ability to notice a difficult emotion more quickly, a useful strategy is noticing the physical sensations in your body. By paying attention to your body, you gain valuable information about your emotions at the earliest possible point.

OUR BODY TELLS THE TRUTH, EVEN BEFORE OUR THINKING BRAIN KNOWS IT.

Fun Fact:

Researchers have found that different emotions are linked with different physical sensations in our bodies. They discovered that different body parts activate (or don't activate) when we are experiencing certain emotions. The more intense the emotion, the more intense the sensation in the body. Pretty cool right?

Take a Minute!

As you read along, start to think about your own intense emotions and make a note of the body sensations you have noticed in yourself. When you notice one of these in your body, check in with yourself about feeling that emotion.

BODY SAYS

EMOTION	HOW DOES IT FEEL? WHAT IS YOUR BODY SAYING?
ANGER	Feeling hot Sweating Faster heartbeat Tension in the arms and hands Tension in the jaw Upward energy, heat, like a volcano Hot energy down through the arms into fists Clenching fists Legs going weak
SADNESS	Tension or lump in throat Heavy heart Chest tightness Quick breathing Stomach churning Teary eyes
SURPRISE	Raised eyebrows Widened mouth Widened eyes Jumping back Screaming Faster heartbeat
DISGUST	Wrinkled nose Curled upper lip Turning away Retching Queasiness
HAPPINESS	Warmth Upward moving energy An urge to reach out and hug someone Smiling Sense of calm in the body
FEAR	Faster heartbeat Chills Numbness in legs Tingling in any body part Fast, shallow breathing Tightened muscles in neck, head, chest, pit of stomach Nausea Sensation of wanting to run/avoid

STEP 2: NAME

Naming an emotion with a word is the second way of helping your thinking brain turn on. The very act of putting a word to an experience slows down your feeling brain and requires your thinking brain to activate. Naming an emotion seems easy at first glance, but a lot of us aren't so great at it. It is important to improve this ability because:

1. Naming an emotion is a complex, higher order brain process, and **WAKES UP THE THINKING BRAIN**.

2. When you name an emotion, you can understand your experience in a more logical way, and it makes it easier to shift your perspective and **GAIN SOME DISTANCE**.

OUR POWER LIES IN CHANGING THE WAY WE RESPOND TO OUR EMOTIONS.

The better you get at noticing and naming your emotions, the better you will be at dealing with them in ways that actually work in your favor and improve your mood. It's a win-win.

There are a ton of words used to name emotions, some negative and some positive. Read through the list on the next page and on page 143 and notice how many words we have in the English language for different emotions. Just reading this list can help improve your ability to name your emotions.

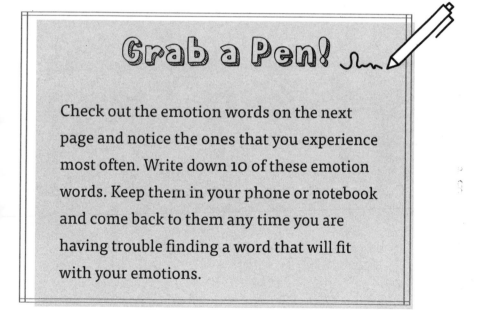

Grab a Pen!

Check out the emotion words on the next page and notice the ones that you experience most often. Write down 10 of these emotion words. Keep them in your phone or notebook and come back to them any time you are having trouble finding a word that will fit with your emotions.

The MOOD WHEEL

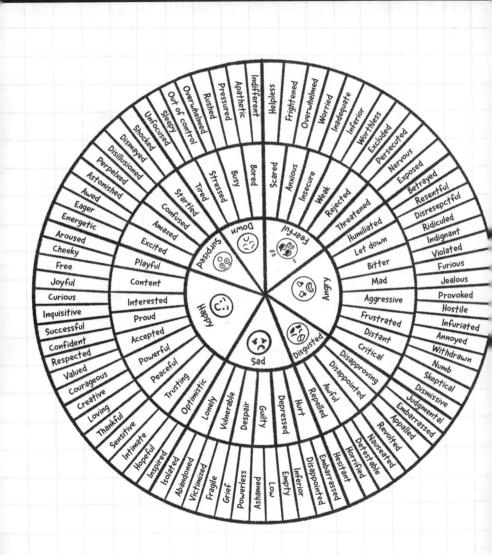

Can't find a word that fits from the Mood Wheel? Sometimes there is no word that seems to describe our emotional experience perfectly, or there are so many emotions happening at the same time that one word just doesn't do it justice.

In these situations, get creative! Think of any descriptive word that feels right, like tangled up inside, squiggles everywhere, mixed up, fluttering, like my body is running a marathon in place. For some of us who are more visual, drawing out what a certain emotion looks like might be super helpful.

Grab a Pen!

Think of a moment in the last few weeks when you felt a strong uncomfortable emotion in your body. Take out a sheet of paper, some pens, crayons, markers, or paint. Think of these questions in your mind as you allow your hand to draw whatever wants to come out: "If my emotion had a physical shape, color, image, what would it look like?" Draw whatever comes to your mind and try not to overthink it! What was this like? Did you learn anything about the emotion that was surprising or new?

STEP 3: ACCEPT

Uncomfortable, unpleasant emotions exist no matter what, and we can't magically make them disappear. But, we can change how we respond and relate to these emotions.

TRYING NOT TO FEEL YOUR EMOTIONS IS PLAYING A LOSING GAME.

There is a difference between noticing an emotion, allowing it to be inside of you, slowing down the process enough to be able to make wiser, less impulsive choices and trying frantically to run from, avoid, or erase that emotion.

The acceptance step of mindfulness means you observe what is going on inside of you with curiosity, without judgment, and without trying to change it. It's the skill of noticing plus just being with your emotional experience.

Mindfulness can be a tough idea to grasp, especially the acceptance step. The goal is to let the emotion be, **GET CURIOUS** about it, without judgment and without trying to change it. This is where the acceptance part comes in. Some tips about practicing mindfulness that you might find helpful as you begin to master these skills are:

- Pretend that you are an observer in a courtroom. You're not the judge, not the jury, not the lawyer, and not the security guard. You have no job to do at all! Your only role is to sit back in the audience and observe the process of your emotions.

- Notice your emotions as if you were watching a movie or tv show. Observe with curiosity without changing the channel or jumping into the screen.

- Imagine a big fire on a TV screen. You can see that it is a fire, you can see that it is hot, you know it is there, but it can't burn you.

- Imagine sitting WITH or NEXT TO the emotion instead of INSIDE of the emotion.

Take a Minute!

Mindful self-talk can also help you sit with a tough emotion when it comes. Here are some of our favorites. Write down at least two or three that resonate with you and keep them in your phone. The next time you are struggling with an emotion or your mood, read them over two to three times to remind you of the goal.

- ☐ I can feel my emotions and be OK.
- ☐ Just be WITH it. Just stay with it.
- ☐ I'll hang with this emotion until it passes.
- ☐ I am uncomfortable and I am safe.
- ☐ What is this emotion trying to say?
- ☐ My power will be back by waiting this out.
- ☐ Emotions are just sensations in my body.
- ☐ I can't control this emotion, but I can slow myself down.
- ☐ Just sit and breathe. My emotions don't control me.
- ☐ Emotions are just energy in motion: they will pass.

TODAY I FEEL...

MINDFULNESS IS BEING ABLE TO NOTICE, GET CURIOUS ABOUT, AND LEARN FROM OUR EMOTIONS WITHOUT TRYING TO CHANGE, ERASE, OR JUDGE THEM.

A Call to Action:

A good starting point to practicing mindfulness is to try to notice your emotions when you are calm and your mood is positive. What emotions are coming up? Can you name them? Can you describe how they feel in your body? What information would they be telling you if they could speak? What color would they be?

Try doing this daily, even for a minute or two, and you will see your skills grow!

Getting to know your emotions and sitting with them will take practice (and a little bit of commitment and work). But you'll get there. Take a look at this real-life example, to see how it could happen for you.

Jacob had been working on lessening the pressure to be "perfect" at school. Come to think of it, Jacob's drive for perfection (which you will learn more about in Chapter 9) was showing up in almost every part of his life, even his friendships. Jacob's best friend Cooper is a very good writer and excels at writing essays for their English class. Jacob had also been getting very good marks on his assignments, but not quite as high as Cooper. For the second week in a row, Jacob asked Cooper how he managed to get 100% on his essays, and Cooper said: "Are you kidding? They're so easy!"

Cooper knew that grades were a sensitive subject for Jacob and that he was really hard on himself when he didn't get the grade he hoped for. But, that day, Cooper spoke before thinking, and without realizing that he may hurt Jacob's feelings. Jacob yelled at Cooper, in the middle of the classroom: "Whatever. You only got 100 because you're the teacher's favorite." Cooper was taken aback and felt mad and hurt. When Jacob got home from school that day, he still felt "off." He regretted his reaction, and wanted to understand what happened, so he went through the three steps of mindfulness.

Jacob remembered noticing a lump in his throat, flushed cheeks, and sweaty hands before yelling at Cooper. His eyes were teary, too. Jacob had a big realization. Based on what he said to Cooper, and how he raised his voice, at the time he had assumed he felt angry, frustrated, and jealous of Cooper.

What he discovered was that the bigger emotions inside of him in that moment were sadness, embarrassment, and shame. Now that he noticed and named his emotions, he knew he had to accept them instead of pretending they weren't there. Although Jacob's instinct was to pretend it was no big deal and act like nothing happened when he saw Cooper the next day, he knew he had to take an action that was consistent with the type of friend he wanted to be (his values!).

Once he asked himself the question: "What can I do that would mean something and help me grow?", the decision was completely clear. Jacob called Cooper that night, told him what he figured out, and said that he was sorry for yelling. Cooper was surprised to find just how much pressure Jacob put on himself in English class and even shared a big mistake he made in another class to make him feel better and get him to laugh. Noticing, naming, accepting, and then taking a helpful action was game-changing for Jacob's mood as well as his friendship with Cooper.

Take a Minute!

Have you ever been in Jacob's position? Or have you been in Cooper's? What do you wish you had done or said differently? Think about how you would like to handle this situation next time.

Take-Away!

Along with your body and thoughts, your emotions play a big part in your mood. There is no such thing as a bad emotion. Of course, some emotions are more comfortable to experience, like joy, happiness, and love, while others can be pretty uncomfortable, like anger, frustration, and shame. Your emotions provide important information about you: what you want, need, enjoy, and what you don't. When you understand your difficult emotions and manage them in healthy ways, you take actions that can help you get out of a negative mood or stay firmly in a positive one.

There is no way to avoid or run from negative emotions, but you can gain some power over your actions by improving your self-regulation skills. Self-regulation is the ability to manage your emotions in ways that improve and balance your mood. One important way to self-regulate is practicing mindfulness, which involves noticing, naming, and accepting your emotions. When you can sit with your emotions without fully jumping into them, you gain the ability to deal with all of life's ups and downs with more ease and balance.

There are times when difficult emotions may get incredibly intense, leading you to take actions that get you stuck in an overwhelmingly negative mood. These moments really test your self-regulation skills, and you may need to use strategies beyond just mindfulness to get back on track. You will learn more about these moments and how to take back your power in these situations in Chapter 10.

Chapter 6

Thinking About Thinking

$\mathcal{H}$ ave you ever thought about what you think? Or why you think the way you do? And how that might all affect your mood? As you might have guessed, what and how you think about something plays an important role in your mood, confidence, and overall wellness. **THOUGHTS ARE POWERFUL**, but you can train your brain to think in more helpful, hopeful, and healthy ways.

The first part of this chapter explains some ways of thinking in response to challenges that come your way, like **global** and **permanent** negative thinking, as well as **internal attribution**. Next, you will read about overall ways of seeing the world, yourself, and others—**core beliefs**. Finally, you'll read about the most common **thinking mistakes** that our brains make when we are stuck in a negative mood.

We all get stuck in negative thinking patterns and make thinking mistakes sometimes, but people who struggle with their mood tend to make them a lot more often. Really!

So keep reading to learn how to spot these thinking patterns and teach your brain to think in ways that are more helpful (and often more realistic). You'll end up in a better place than where you started, with loads more balance and confidence.

YOU CAN CHANGE THE WAY YOU FEEL BY CHANGING THE WAY YOU THINK!

INTERNAL ATTRIBUTION, GLOBAL, AND PERMANENT NEGATIVE THINKING

When you are stuck in a negative mood or emotional funk, you might blame yourself for bad situations and tell yourself there is nothing you can change about it. You think challenges or problems are everywhere, will last forever, and are entirely your fault. And you think good things or successes won't last, rarely happen, or that you just got lucky.

People who struggle with their mood usually view **CHALLENGES** as wide reaching, permanent, and all their fault. Thinking that any set back is entirely your fault, is called "internal attribution."

Here is an example of a time when Maria got stuck in this type of negative thinking pattern after experiencing a set-back:

Maria getting a C- on her geometry test was rough! So if the goal is to think about the negative experience as a one-time, unique, temporary situation that doesn't really mean anything beyond its initial moment, how do you do it? How can you start to think differently so that you can improve your mood?

After Maria got a C- on her Geometry test, here's how her thoughts sounded. She thought...

	Specific	Global
Temporary	One subject is very hard for me. This year I'm bad at geometry.	I'm really bad at school this year. I am a failure at everything this week.
Permanent	I will always suck at math! I will never improve.	I am a failure! Period. Full stop. I will never succeed at school or life.

None of these thoughts are super positive, but can you guess which ones felt a little less yucky? Can you tell which thoughts made her feel the worst?

This is the yucky place to be stuck! Maria focused on several negative thoughts, but some made her feel worse than others.

Here's how Maria could think in a more helpful way. The goal is to shift thinking back to any other square and BONUS points if you can land on the top left square (**Specific, Temporary** Thinking).

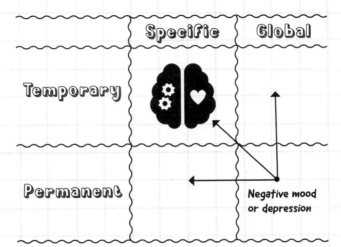

	Specific	Global
Temporary		
Permanent		Negative mood or depression

Maria would have felt better by shifting her **global and permanent** thought into any of the other boxes, making her tough experience feel more tied to a particular moment and activity instead of tied to everything in her life and lasting forever. Maria also blamed herself completely for her test grade instead of looking at the whole picture (remember internal attribution?). To feel better, Maria could try to see the event in context:

- I could have prepared more, but this was a very challenging test.

- I should have spent a bit more time studying, but I also know my teacher is a tough grader. See how small changes in attribution can make a big difference?

Jacob has been feeling down lately, and today's math class was no exception. Though his teacher pointed out a few things that Jacob did well, Jacob kept focusing on a homework question that he just couldn't get right.

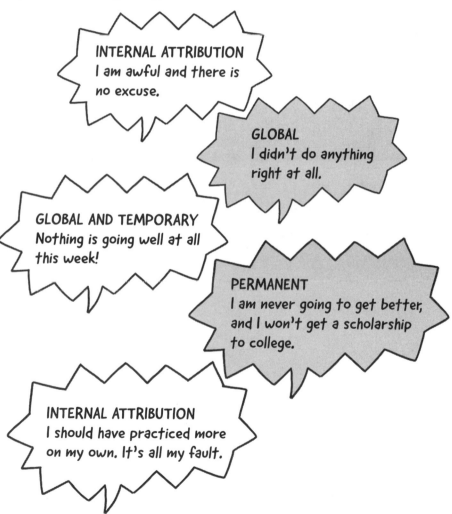

INTERNAL ATTRIBUTION
I am awful and there is no excuse.

GLOBAL
I didn't do anything right at all.

GLOBAL AND TEMPORARY
Nothing is going well at all this week!

PERMANENT
I am never going to get better, and I won't get a scholarship to college.

INTERNAL ATTRIBUTION
I should have practiced more on my own. It's all my fault.

Not surprisingly, Jacob felt awful after class and even the rest of that week. Because he was so down, it was hard to put a lot of effort in at school the next day and he avoided talking to his friends. All of this just built up and made him feel even worse.

When something challenging happens, a great strategy is to **PURPOSELY CHANGE** some of these wide-reaching, permanent, and self-blaming or internally attributed thoughts to ones that are more specific, temporary, and honor the bigger picture or full context. Try to imagine these new thoughts standing out in bold lettering or speaking to you more loudly. Here are some examples of thoughts that Jacob came up with. These thoughts are probably more reasonable and definitely more helpful.

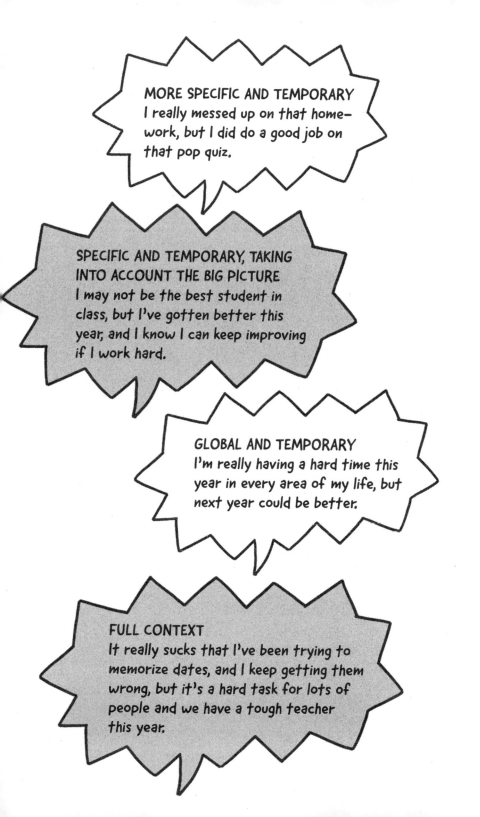

Grab a Pen! ✒️

Imagine a moment in the last few weeks when you were having a tough time. Maybe you felt hopeless, helpless, or insecure? Pick one of these moments to focus on. What were you saying to yourself about YOU? What would your thoughts be if you saw this challenge as temporary, as only affecting one part of your life, and as not entirely your fault? What might you say to yourself instead? What more helpful thought could you turn up the volume on?

NEGATIVE CORE BELIEFS

What is the big deal with global, permanent, and self-blaming thinking? As if it wasn't enough that this type of thinking contributes to a negative mood, thinking this way over time can contribute to feelings of low self-worth, lack of confidence, and even more importantly, leaves you holding on to negative, unhelpful core beliefs about yourself and everything around you. Core beliefs are deeply-held assumptions we make about the world and ourselves, and they affect the way we interact with others.

Some core beliefs can be so deeply held that you don't even realize you have them! This can be pretty problematic when those core beliefs are negative. You're not born with negative core beliefs; you learn them throughout your life based on the ways in which you think about your experiences. These deep, negative thoughts can lead to a lot of additional challenges, including trouble trusting others, feeling self-conscious and insecure in relationships, putting others' needs above your own, low self-esteem, anxiety, and depression.

Take a Minute!

On page 159 there is a list of negative core beliefs. Can you think of any more that you or your friends have? Think of some of the reasons you or they may have these beliefs. Did anything specific happen to you or them? Were you or they put in a situation with a negative outcome? Ask yourself if this core belief is telling the **full** story of who you or they are.

Jacob was pretty confident in a lot of areas of his life, but when he struggled in his math class, he noticed that he was holding on to the idea that he was "worthless." Each time  his parents tried to help him with homework, he got frustrated with them, then guilty about his anger, and "I am worthless" became even louder. Jacob wanted to believe that he was worthy of happiness even if he isn't great at math. He wrote down "I am worthy even if I'm not a math wizard" and repeated it every time he sat down to do math homework. It made him laugh a bit each time, and over time, he was able to see himself as worthy and his mood during class improved.

THE GOOD NEWS IS, JUST BY TEACHING YOUR BRAIN TO THINK DIFFERENTLY, YOU CAN SHIFT THESE NEGATIVE CORE BELIEFS, FEEL A WHOLE LOT BETTER ABOUT YOURSELF (AND ABOUT EVERYTHING ELSE FOR THAT MATTER), AND IMPROVE YOUR MOOD.

NEGATIVE
Core Beliefs

BELIEFS ABOUT MYSELF	BELIEFS ABOUT OTHERS	BELIEFS ABOUT THE WORLD
HELPLESS		
I am weak.	I need others to feel good.	Nothing good ever happens.
I am a loser.	People don't care about what I have to say.	Life is always hard.
I am trapped.	Nobody understands me.	Everything is out of my control.
UNLOVABLE		
I am unlovable.	No one will like me if they get to know me.	The world is hard for people like me.
I will end up alone.	People will always end up ditching me.	The world is a tough place for people like me.
No one likes me.	Other people are more likable than me.	Life is full of people better than me.
WORTHLESS		
I am bad.	Others are better than me.	Life won't go my way.
I don't deserve to live.	Others are more deserving of joy.	My life sucks.
I am worthless.	Other people will never want me.	I don't deserve a happy life.
SAFETY		
I am not safe.	People can't be trusted.	The world is dangerous.
Feeling good is not ok.	Others will always betray me.	Things never go well for me.
I need to hide my feelings.	People are out to get me.	Life is unfair.

Changing negative core beliefs is not easy. It is tricky to spot them sometimes, because they are usually hidden underneath our daily, more obvious thoughts, and our brains typically ignore information that could contradict these negative beliefs. But if you have gotten this far in reading this book, I know you are someone who can do hard things! All it takes is continued practice and a willingness to grow and learn even when you get knocked down.

Grab a Pen!

Which negative core beliefs do you relate to most? Write down two or three healthy beliefs that you would like to have instead. How did it feel to write these down? Keep these healthy core beliefs in your phone or notebook and say them to yourself (out loud or in your mind) every morning (not just when you are feeling down). The more your brain notices you saying these positive statements about yourself on purpose, the easier it will be for your brain to generate these thoughts automatically. If you get stuck, take a look at the next page for some ideas.

HEALTHY Core Beliefs

BELIEFS ABOUT MYSELF	BELIEFS ABOUT OTHERS	BELIEFS ABOUT THE WORLD
CAPABLE		
I am strong.	Others will be there for me.	Life has ups and downs.
I am able.	Most people have good intentions.	Life can be hard but also great!
I am capable.	People are not perfect.	I can control some things and not others.
LOVABLE		
I am enough.	Not everyone will like me and that's ok.	Life has meaning even when it's hard.
I am lovable.	Some people will love me and others will not.	Life can be complicated at times, and that's okay.
I deserve care and love.	People are all different.	Life is full of pain and also joy.
WORTHY		
I am a good person.	I can't compare myself to others.	Some things won't go my way, and others will.
I am trying.	People have strengths and weaknesses.	My life has its ups and downs.
I am worthy.	Some people will like me and others won't.	I deserve a happy life.
SAFETY		
I am safe.	I can listen to my intuition.	There is danger but also safety in the world.
I can handle feeling uncomfortable.	Others can be kind.	If I try hard, I know I will succeed.
Feelings are information.	People mean well, even when they make mistakes.	Some things in life are not fair, and I can accept that.

THINKING MISTAKES

We all make thinking mistakes on a daily basis. Yes, even cognitive-behavioral therapists like me! These ways of thinking become a problem when they happen often, and when you have a hard time being flexible in shifting them as your brain takes in new information to contradict or challenge them. When it comes to negative moods, the most common thinking mistakes are **zooming in, self-blame,** and **mind-reading.**

ZOOMING IN. Sometimes this thinking mistake is also called "filtering" or "ignoring the good." When your brain is making this type of thinking mistake, you are paying more attention to the bad things that are happening than anything else that is going on. At the same time, you are ignoring or dismissing anything that is positive, or even neutral.

Here are some examples of how people zoom in on the negative:

- Maria got one C- in her Math class and it was all that she could think about. She was zooming in on one grade and ignoring the rest of her grades that whole semester.

- Jacob scored one goal, but all he could focus on was the shot that he missed. He was zooming in on the missed opportunity and barely noticed that he helped win the game.

- Casey often zoomed in on how sad it was that their parents got divorced. They just couldn't get their mind off of it and kept thinking "my life sucks now." Meanwhile,  the fact that they were feeling really close to their friends, were succeeding as debate captain, and still had a good relationship with each of their parents kept getting out of focus.

- Maria scored an 89 on a history quiz and kept focusing on self-critical thoughts about this grade, which was fairly low for her. Meanwhile, her mind completely  skipped over the fact that, even with this quiz grade, her overall grade in history was still a 99.

- Jacob hung out with his friends almost every weekend, but his brain was getting stuck on the one time his best friend Rob didn't respond to his texts over one weekend. His brain was ignoring all of the  times that Rob did text him, and also the times when he himself would forget to write back.

Can you think of one time where your brain zoomed in on the negative?

 **SELF-BLAMING.** Self-blame happens when you blame yourself for anything that goes wrong around you, even if you had nothing to do with it. It's when you take more responsibility for a negative situation or negative outcome than you should.

Let's see how Casey and Maria tended to self-blame around several things in their lives.

- Every time Casey thought about their parents' divorce, they thought about all of the things that they may have done to increase their parents' stress and ruin their relationship. In reality, their parents' relationship had nothing at all to do with them, and in fact, their dad and mom were actually much happier since their separation.

- Maria tended to blame herself for any drama that happened in her friend group or family. One time, two of her friends took friendly teasing a little too far when they hurt her

brother's feelings while hanging out at Maria's house. Although Maria noticed and defended her brother, she couldn't shake the thoughts "I'm such a bad sister, it's all my fault" and "I should have stopped them sooner." In reality, there is no way she could have predicted her brother's reaction or her friends' teasing.

ALTHOUGH IT'S ALWAYS GOOD TO TAKE ACCOUNTABILITY FOR THE ROLE WE HAVE PLAYED IN A DIFFICULT SITUATION OR SETBACK, SELF-BLAMING ISN'T PAINTING THE FULL PICTURE OR TELLING THE WHOLE STORY.

There are many things that can impact tricky situations and mistakes, and self-blaming doesn't do justice to the context in which our behavior takes place.

Take a Minute!

What are some things that you tend to blame yourself for? Can you relate to Casey or Maria? Do you know a friend or family member who struggles a lot with self-blame?

ANOTHER TYPE OF THINKING MISTAKE IS MIND READING.

Mind-reading usually includes a few different thinking mistakes all wrapped into one. One is that your thoughts are telling you that you can know what someone else is thinking. Second, your thoughts are telling you that other people are noticing and thinking about you often or all the time.

The truth is, unless you are psychic (more power to you!), you can't possibly see into other people's minds and know what is in there. And in general, we humans are pretty focused on ourselves. We are usually busy thinking about what we need to do, making a mental checklist, worrying about our future, thinking about our relationships or what we will eat for our next meal, or what our favorite flavor of ice cream is. Lastly, mind-reading leads you to think that other people are always thinking negative things about you, the way you look, talk, or act. This may be true SOME of the time, but again, it's not painting the full and complete picture. Let's look at some evidence:

Jacob often caught himself mind-reading; thinking that his classmates were noticing and judging his every word and action. To test out the accuracy of his assumption, he wrote down all of the thoughts running through his mind during class to see how many were focused on others in a negative light.

(S) **(—)** I'm hungry and I wish this class would just end already.

(O) **(—)** Nicole looks like she isn't paying attention.

(O) **(—)** I really don't like Cooper's new backpack. It's too bright of a green.

(S) **(X)** I have to start paying attention if I want to get the highest grade in the class again.

(S) **(—)** I have to get into AP chemistry next year or I will literally die.

(O) **(X)** The person behind me is chewing gum so loud. Gross.

(S) **(—)** Summer is coming so soon, maybe I can call my aunt to plan a pool day at her house soon.

(S) **(✓)** Thank goodness the sun came out today, that way I can study outside later.

(S) **(—)** I should probably eat my lunch in a classroom so I can focus on starting my homework.

(O) **(X)** This class is moving too slow, why do people keep asking questions? Just move on!

(X) Negative   **(—)** Neutral   **(✓)** Positive   **(O)** Others   **(S)** Self

Take a Minute!

What were you thinking when you read Jacob's thoughts? You probably have hundreds of thoughts running through your mind during just one class. Some are probably focused on others, some are focused on you, and some are focused on neutral things like the weather, your plans, food, or random facts that pop up in your brain. This is just what the brain does. When you mind-read, your mind is painting a picture that is often way more negative and centered on you than reality is.

NOBODY IS SPENDING EVERY MOMENT THINKING ABOUT YOU

 How can I tell if I'm making a thinking mistake, and what do I do about it?

There are a few strategies that can help you catch your brain when it is not telling you the full truth (or the truth at all). The next time you suspect that your thoughts might be thinking mistakes, ask yourself these three questions to help you decide:

1. Is this thought 100% true?

2. Is this thought fully true 100% of the time?

3. Would most people find this thought fully true 100% of the time?

If you answer no to any of the above, chances are your brain is caught up in a thinking mistake.

To get unstuck, pause and ask yourself:

1. What would be a more helpful way of thinking about this?

2. How would someone with a lot of confidence be thinking about this?

Take-Away!

In this chapter, we looked at the important role that your thinking patterns play in your mood, confidence, and overall wellness.

Thoughts are incredibly powerful, and you can change how you feel by changing the way that you think.

Some general thinking patterns that get us stuck in a negative mood (and keep us down there) happen when we attribute negative events to internal, stable, and global factors, while attributing positive events to external, temporary, and specific factors. We end up thinking that problems are everywhere, will last forever, and are caused entirely by us, while thinking that positive events or successes won't last, rarely happen, and are caused by something outside of us. Negative thinking also contributes to a type of powerful thought pattern we develop about ourselves called a negative core belief. When our core beliefs are negative, it is very hard to maintain a sense of confidence and joy.

I also talked about some common thinking mistakes associated with negative moods, including zooming in on the negative, self-blame, and mind-reading. When you can notice these mistakes and practice coming up with thoughts that are more reasonable and helpful, you can change your mood and the way you feel about yourself.

Now that you practiced some positive thinking skills, and learned a few new ways of talking to yourself, you are on your way to feeling so much better. If you keep intentionally and regularly practicing positive self-talk, your mood and confidence will soar.

Chapter 7

Mood and Mindset

*N*ow that you understand how much power your thoughts have over your emotions and mood, let's take that one step further. I am talking about changing your **mindset**—your overall thinking strategy about yourself, your life, your relationships and your goals. **YOUR MINDSET IS EVERYTHING!** And you guessed it, thinking patterns core beliefs, and thinking mistakes contribute to the type of mindsets you develop.

Your mindset makes a huge difference in your mood, and you can learn how to use the power of mindset to your advantage in creating the life you want. The most damaging mindsets when it comes to our mood are a **self-criticism mindset, a fixed mindset**, and a **deprivation mindset**. But the truth is you can change your mood and beliefs about yourself by practicing a **growth mindset, self-compassion,** and **gratitude**. The result? A better mood, more joy, and way more confidence.

Take a Minute!

Do you know anyone who seems to roll with the punches and never gets stuck in a dark mental space? Do you know someone whose life situation is very challenging, but they actually seem....happy? Can you think of someone who has fewer outside resources than you (talent, support, popularity, money) and still manages to achieve their goals without getting discouraged?

Think of a person like this. It can be someone you know or a fictional character, as long as it's someone who keeps facing obstacles, failures, and hardships, and never gives up. Ask around if you can't think of anyone. Guaranteed, the path to success for this person is their mindset.

DIGGING A LITTLE DEEPER INTO MINDSET...

Your mindset is a general frame of mind, mental attitude, or way of thinking that is created over time. As you go through your life, you collect sets of thoughts and beliefs based on your experiences and perceptions. This is a big deal. Your mindset directly impacts how you think, what you feel, and how you act. The most important thing to remember here is that **MINDSET IS CHANGEABLE**. That's right: a helpful mindset is not something you are born with or without, it is something that you learn, and therefore can learn to shift over time to your advantage. You're not stuck with it!

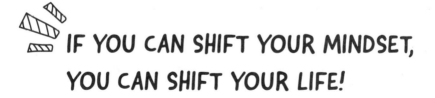 **IF YOU CAN SHIFT YOUR MINDSET, YOU CAN SHIFT YOUR LIFE!**

We will look at three types of mindsets that are deeply relevant to your mood, emotions, actions, and success:

- growth mindset vs. fixed mindset
- deprivation mindset vs. gratitude mindset
- self-criticism vs. self-compassion

GROWTH MINDSET VS. FIXED MINDSET

When someone has a **fixed mindset**, they believe that their intelligence, talent, and skills are unchangeable, or fixed. An example would be the belief that you are either smart at math or not. You are good at writing or not. People in a fixed mindset accept their current ability or circumstances as permanent and do not try to grow these abilities or shift their situation. In fact, they tend to give up when something is really hard or doesn't come easily.

When someone has a **growth mindset**, they believe that they can improve most of their abilities with dedication and hard work. For example, the belief that you can become excellent at math by putting in the effort and working hard at it. Or if you keep writing and revising your essay, your words will shine. People in a growth mindset view their natural talent and life circumstances as just a starting point and believe that real accomplishment can be achieved if they keep learning and growing. Having a growth mindset helps us develop two qualities that are helpful in life: resilience and a desire to learn.

How do I build a growth mindset?

SHIFT YOUR ACTIONS! A great starting point is to "act" like someone with a growth mindset. Challenge yourself and take some risks in areas of your life that matter to you: trying out for a sport, choosing a challenging but interesting academic subject, starting a new project like film making, or connecting with your friends and community. Pick something that doesn't come easily or naturally to you, dedicate time to learning how to improve, and work hard at it without giving up. This sounds counter-intuitive, but a growth mindset requires you to be curious about your mistakes, to enjoy your effort, and never stop learning. Take pride in your journey and appreciate the good effort you put forth to reach your goal instead of focusing only on the actual goal or accomplishment itself. The next step in building a growth mindset lies in shifting your thinking.

Take a Minute!

Think about your day so far or yesterday. Ask yourself these three questions: What did I learn? What mistake that I made taught me something? What did I try hard at?

SHIFT YOUR SELF-TALK! The next way of achieving a growth mindset is to think like someone with a growth mindset. On purpose. Write down some thoughts consistent with a growth mindset and read them every day. The very act of reading and writing turns on your thinking brain, and makes it easier to see things clearly. By writing and reading positive self-talk statements, you are also **RE-WIRING YOUR BRAIN AND CREATING NEW NEURAL PATHWAYS** (remember neuroplasticity?).

Even if you don't believe these self-talk statements just yet, even if they feel fake, just the act of reading or coming up with them is making it easier for your brain to generate these types of thoughts on its own in the future. Fake it 'til you make it! Instead of treating your negative, fixed mindset thoughts as untrue or bad, think of practicing positive self-talk as a way of adding more thoughts to your brain's narrative.

Over time, your brain will start generating growth mindset thoughts on its own, and you will feel so much better. As you continue to practice thinking this way on purpose, it will stop feeling forced, and become a natural part of who you are.

Here are some examples:

INSTEAD OF THIS...	TRY THIS...
This was way too hard, and I don't want to do it again. I am clearly not good at it. →	If something takes a lot of effort, it means it is important to me and I was willing to work for it.
Did I win? Did I lose? →	Did I give my best effort at least one time at one moment?
I can't run fast enough to make the team, so what's the point in trying? →	I can't run fast enough YET, but I can keep training so that I have a chance to play next year.
I'm not taking advanced creative writing, it's just too hard and I'll never get the grade I want. →	I can think of taking creative writing as a way to challenge myself and maybe have fun. Being willing and enjoying myself is more important than getting an A.
I'm not athletic, so even though my friends are all playing softball, there is no way I'm trying out. →	It's important enough to be with my friends that I am willing to put myself out there.

DEPRIVATION MINDSET VS GRATITUDE MINDSET

When you are in a **deprivation mindset**, your thoughts tell you that you are not important or lovable, and you feel as if you never have enough of the things you want and need. When you focus on this kind of scarcity in several areas of your life, such as in relationships, academic life, sports, and family life, you'll end up feeling depressed, helpless, anxious, stuck, and unmotivated. You've unintentionally deprived yourself of anything that's good! How can you stay in a balanced, positive mood, when you are focusing on all the things you don't have, can't do, won't succeed at, and miss out on? Think you might be getting stuck in a deprivation mindset? Here are some questions to reflect on:

- Do you never feel like you have enough time to do the things you need to (or want to) do?

- Do you always think about how few friends you have, instead of thinking about the connections you **do** have?

- Do you focus more on what you can't do than what you **can**?

- Do you often compare yourself to those around you who have things you wish you had?

- Do you often use words like "I can't, I won't, I don't"?

- Do you focus on your failures more than your successes?

- Do you get stuck thinking about all your mistakes and missed opportunities?

Just like the other mindsets in this chapter, a **gratitude mindset** can be created and grown by practicing being appreciative in specific ways on purpose. When you are in a gratitude mindset, your mind is focused on the opportunities around you, and you are zooming in on what you already have. Even when you are feeling down, facing a disappointment, or experiencing a serious hardship, there are opportunities all around you to find thankfulness. Shifting your focus to these opportunities gives you a chance to feel lighter even in a storm of heaviness.

A gratitude mindset allows you to focus your brain on the positive things in your life rather than the negative, the wins rather than the losses, the things that make you feel joy instead of sadness. As you develop and practice this mindset, you will feel more self-confidence, happiness, and acceptance, plus less stress and negativity. When you are practicing gratitude, your experiences are enhanced, your relationships are stronger, and even your health and well-being can improve. People who **intentionally practice gratitude** can manage tough events, situations, and feelings with more ease.

PRO TIP

There will always be someone in your life who is better than you, smarter than you, better looking, has a body that more closely resembles our culture's narrow ideal (don't get me started), has more friends, and is more creative. The growth of social media has made our tendency to compare ourselves to others so much harder to avoid. Also remember, as you are focusing on someone who you think is better than you, there is someone focusing on how you are better than them! There is always going to be someone better than you at a certain thing, no matter where you fall on the imaginary scale of "who's best?" The gratitude mindset offers protection against this as it takes you out of comparison mode and puts you into enjoying the wonderful parts of you and your own life.

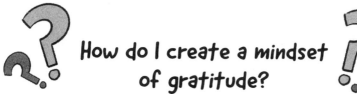

How do I create a mindset of gratitude?

The best way to grow your gratitude muscle is to practice being grateful, on purpose, in small ways every single day. Here are some strategies that can help:

- **INTENTIONALLY** focus on what is good about your life (people, sense of community, supportive family, achievements, health, ability to move and exercise, access to yummy food). Find things to savor!

- **DON'T COMPARE** yourself to others. Period.

- **BE MINDFUL** with your social media use—choose to follow accounts that make you feel good and unfollow those that bring you down.

- **BE THOUGHTFUL** about how much time you spend staring at the screen.

Not-So-Fun Fact:

Too much social media use has been found to increase symptoms of depression, anxiety, and negative body image.

PRO TIP

Social media photos and stories are specifically created to portray an image of what someone wants to look like or wants to feel. They are not the truth.

Be cautious of how much time you spend looking at other people on social media: I'm not asking you to never scroll through Instagram, but I am saying "pay attention" to the story your mind is telling you about what you are seeing. If we focus on these things, we lose track of all of the internal qualities that we possess ourselves.

DON'T COMPARE YOUR TRUE SELF TO EVERYBODY ELSE'S EXTERNAL IMAGE.

PRACTICE GRATITUDE SELF-TALK. Try writing these down or keeping them in your phone for moments when you need some inspiration.

- I can't do everything, but I can do something.

- Every failure is a problem to be faced, dealt with, and learned from.

- I am choosing to focus on growth over perfection.

- When I am grateful, fear disappears, and opportunity appears.

- What *can* my body and mind do?

- I may not have everything I want, but I have everything I need.

- Focus on what I have instead of what I don't.

- I can focus on my power to notice and enjoy all that is special and meaningful in my life.

A Call to Action:

Every evening, write down three things that you are grateful for from that day. Try to make these things different from the night before and ask yourself, "What went well today? What was right about today? Which moment am I proud of?" Start tonight and continue for two weeks. Notice that it feels more natural and easy over time.

Lastly, try catching yourself when you notice words that might signal a deprivation mindset and change your approach. Here are some common examples.

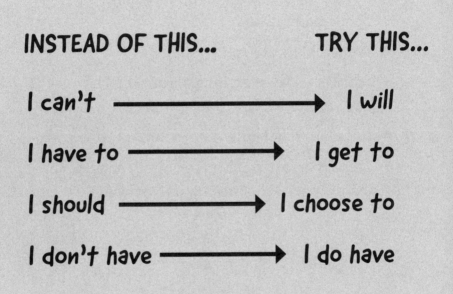

INSTEAD OF THIS...		TRY THIS...
I can't	⟶	I will
I have to	⟶	I get to
I should	⟶	I choose to
I don't have	⟶	I do have

SELF-CRITICISM MINDSET VS SELF-COMPASSION MINDSET

You've already learned how self-blame and a negative core belief about yourself can lead to a longstanding bad mood. A **self-critical mindset** is like self-blame on steroids. When we are in this mindset, all we can see are our mistakes, faults, and weaknesses. All we can think about is picking out the things we don't like in ourselves, and a core belief of being a "failure" or "not good enough" runs through seemingly every part of our lives.

 **Do you tend to dwell on your mistakes or think you are not good enough?**

This section of the chapter could be life-changing for you. Not surprisingly, when your thinking patterns create this mindset, you can feel pretty awful, insecure, and what's more, unmotivated. When you are stuck in a self-critical mindset, you are less likely to achieve your goals, and you definitely feel worse emotionally.

 **Have you been holding onto the belief that you have to be hard on yourself in order to succeed?**

Jacob was worried about letting go of some of his self-critical thoughts. His fear was that if he changed to a more compassionate mindset, he would not achieve the goals he set out for himself: get into a top-tier school, and graduate as valedictorian.

Jacob's misconception is common! The cold hard truth is this: self-critical thinking is way less effective at increasing motivation and performance than self-compassion. Being too hard on yourself can actually decrease your success. Not convinced? Check out the box on page 194 about all the research backing this information up.

A **self-compassion mindset** is all about balancing self-acceptance with self-improvement. It is more than just kindness and warm fuzzy emotions. It combines accepting and having empathy for yourself and taking a realistic view of yourself and your actions.

A self-compassion mindset has three main parts:

- **SELF-KINDNESS:** using kinder, gentler words towards ourselves
- **COMMON HUMANITY:** a sense that pain and failures are a universal part of life and experienced by all humans

- **MINDFULNESS:** noticing your emotions with curiosity, and without jumping into, or judging them

A self-compassion mindset allows you to use kind words towards yourself during times of failure or pain, feel "part of" or connected to others, accept the ups and downs of life, and have empathy for your mistakes. People who are in a self-compassion mindset are more motivated, happier, more optimistic, feel better about their bodies, and have a higher sense of self-worth. Seriously, there is so much scientific research to support this!

Not only does a self-compassion mindset foster all of these positive feelings, it increases your **grit:** that is, your ability to get through rough times and overcome adversity. Last, but not least, a self-compassion mindset improves your mood, protects you from the harmful effects of stress, and decreases anxiety and depression.

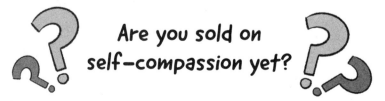

Are you sold on self-compassion yet?

PRO TIP

Researchers have found lots of interesting information about self-criticism and self-compassion when it comes to success, motivation, and performance. Study after study has shown that self-compassion motivates people to improve themselves and perform more effectively. Here are just a few findings.

- People spent more time studying for a hard test after an initial failure and reported greater motivation to change their weaknesses when they practiced self-compassion.

- People with high levels of self-compassion reported more happiness, joy, wisdom, personal initiative, curiosity, exploration, agreeableness, extroversion, conscientiousness, and fewer negative feelings and emotional struggles.

- People who scored higher on tests of self-compassion had higher feelings of self-worth, and this self-worth was more stable. People who scored lower on tests of self-compassion reported more negative mood states, self-consciousness, and anger.

SELF-CRITICAL THINKING IS WAY LESS EFFECTIVE AT INCREASING MOTIVATION AND PERFORMANCE THAN SELF-COMPASSION.

BUILD YOUR SELF-COMPASSION MUSCLES

The overall idea in shifting from a self-critical to a self-compassion mindset is to **SPEAK TO YOURSELF THE WAY THAT YOU WOULD SPEAK TO SOMEONE YOU LOVE.** Think of it like this: you are trying to coach yourself through setbacks, or life's ups and downs, the way that you would be coached by a super supportive, inspirational, but also tough coach. You know the kind of mentor that tells you the truth, helps you improve your weaknesses, and celebrates your strengths with you? That's who we want you to channel. Not a coach that is always pointing out flaws, tearing people down, and making players feel bad about themselves. And definitely not like your sibling who is always making fun of you, or that bully that has been teasing you all semester.

LET'S PRACTICE CREATING A SELF-COMPASSIONATE MINDSET.

Grab a Pen! ✒️

Pick a moment when you were feeling down and really badly about yourself in the last few weeks. Try to remember what you were saying about yourself and to yourself. Go back to that moment in your mind, shift your energy, and write down the answers to the questions below:

- ☐ What would you say to a friend you care about?
- ☐ What would one of your closest friends say to you?
- ☐ What would you say to yourself if you lean into the wisest, most compassionate part of you (even if it only makes up 5% of you)?
- ☐ What would your most inspiring mentor be saying to themselves in that moment?

A Call to Action:

Next time a friend is feeling down, try to remember what you said or did to help them feel better. Try saying this exact thing to yourself at a later time, when you feel stuck trying to give yourself compassion.

Though you can't rely only on inspirational quotes to instantly create a self-compassionate mindset, the ones that resonate with you can help you shift and re-focus when you are feeling stuck. The right mantra can get you back on track in a deep and meaningful way over time.

Here are some of my favorites:

- I don't have to be perfect to be perfectly worthy.
- Struggle is part of life.
- I'm having a hard time right now and that's ok.
- May I be kind to myself in this moment.
- I am flawed and make mistakes, and that is ok.
- I am not a bad person, I am a person having a hard time.
- My struggles and imperfections don't define me.
- I am at peace with who I am.
- It makes perfect sense that I did that.
- I will give myself love and compassion.
- I will not be ashamed of my story.
- It's not about what I have or haven't achieved, it is about who I am on the inside.

- I can accept my weaknesses just as much as I accept my strengths.
- I am going to be ok. Things will work out, even if not perfectly.
- Everybody makes mistakes, turns out I'm a human, too.
- Everybody goes through a rough patch.
- Life is about the moments when no one is watching.

A Call to Action:

Do you have any favorite movie or TV show quotes? Song lyrics that you find lift you up? Try to think of some that help you feel self-compassion, add them to the list above, and keep it in your phone or notebook. Do you have a talent for art? Take this a step further and get crafty. Make a collage of the lyrics or quotes and hang them somewhere you can see when you need it the most—on your bedroom wall, in your locker, tucked away in the notebook of your hardest class.

Do you remember some of Jacob's self-critical thoughts? To start creating a more self-compassionate mindset, he came up with a few go-to statements to remind him of his worth:

- There are many things that are valuable about me in addition to my academic performance.

- It is ok to not be the best person in the class every single day.

- It's hard to feel so much academic pressure, how can I take care of myself in a deeper way?

Take-Away!

Mindset is an overall way of approaching yourself, others, your goals, and your circumstances. Thinking patterns, thinking mistakes, and core beliefs all shape your mindset, meaning your mindset is learned based on your life experiences. This is great news, because it means you can do things to shift your mindset so that you feel happier, more confident, and more balanced in the face of life's ups and downs.

In this chapter, you learned just how much of a difference mindset makes in your mood, and how to use the power of mindset to your advantage in creating the life you want. The mindsets that are most damaging to your mood and wellbeing are a fixed mindset, a self-critical mindset, and a deprivation mindset. With intention and practice, you can develop a mindset of growth, self-compassion, and gratitude instead. Not only are these approaches shown to increase happiness, joy, and confidence, but they also help you achieve the goals that are important to you.

Some strategies and words to remember on your journey to a more empowering mindset:

 Take actions that those with a growth mindset would take (even if you feel afraid or uncertain).

Talk to yourself like someone with a self-compassion mindset would talk to themselves.

Remind yourself that your failures are opportunities for learning and growth.

Intentionally notice moments you are grateful for at the end of each day, no matter how small.

Treat setbacks and obstacles like an invitation to rise to the challenge.

Be an inspiring mentor to yourself.

Chapter 8

Perfectionism ≠ Self-Love

$\mathcal{N}$ ow for a thinking style that deserves its very own chapter: **PERFECTIONISM**.

Yup, the pressure to be perfect. This is different from other types of thinking mistakes, core beliefs, and mindsets in that it is so misunderstood.

Many people believe they can only achieve self-love, confidence, and a positive mood if they are perfect and everything around them is perfect, too. Lots of people credit their academic, career, social, athletic, relationship, and creative success to being perfect. Time to debunk this myth!

The constant pressure and need to be perfect is exhausting. And it's just not that helpful to you in the long run. Instead of perfectionism, the most accurate predictors of success and positive mood are **FLEXIBILITY, GRIT,** and **CONFIDENCE**.

Seriously.

Face it. A perfectionistic mindset may not be working for you, or at least not fully and all of the time. Instead, you can have this type of deep confidence and true self-love without the relentless need for perfection. Real confidence, the kind that radiates out of a person as soon as you meet them, and no matter what they are going through, has to do with an internally-generated sense of self-worth.

Translation: **YOU WILL ONLY FIND SELF-LOVE AND CONFIDENCE INSIDE OF YOU, NOT OUTSIDE OF YOU.**

After reading this chapter, you will have traveled a good distance on your own journey to more flexible thinking, a more balanced view of yourself, a deeper self-love, and a positive mood and energy. You might just learn that the things that make you so valuable and worthy have actually been inside of you all along. It's worth the effort to take a look, so let's get started.

 What is most valuable about you shines through when no one is watching. Who do you want to be in those moments?

PERFECTIONISM

You have heard this word many times and are probably familiar with what perfectionistic thoughts and actions look like. What you may not know is that perfectionism can actually get in the way of not only your joy and positive mood, but also your achievements and life goals. That's right. Many of the messages that we hear throughout our lives make it seem like a perfectionistic mindset is the one and only factor, or the most important factor, in achieving success (whatever your idea of success is). This is not the full truth, not even close.

THE TRUTH IS THAT FLEXIBILITY, GRIT, AND CONFIDENCE are the key ingredients in progress, productivity, academic and career success, healthy relationships, and a balanced, positive mood.

In fact, a perfectionistic mindset has a seriously ugly side. It is one of the most common thinking patterns associated with stress, externally focused sense of self-worth (more about this later), negative mood, and depression. No matter which way you slice it, perfectionism naturally traps us in a self-critical mindset. You already know how unhelpful that is!

Perfectionistic thinking can get many people stuck in a whirlwind of procrastination, self-blame, guilt, and shame. Not surprisingly, this can leave you in a negative mood.

Just how does a perfectionistic mindset do this? Like other thinking mistakes and negative thinking styles, perfectionism feeds into a loop of negative thoughts, feelings, and actions which then reinforce each other. Perfectionistic thinking leads you to set extremely high, and sometimes unrealistic standards for yourself and others. When these standards are so high, and so inflexible, you end up falling short of these goals much of the time (and so do others). You end up disappointed in yourself or in others way too often.

Perfectionistic expectations
of your performance

↘

you don't meet your expectations

↘

disappointment & shame

↘

even stronger need for more perfectionistic
goals to try to feel better

↘

EXHAUSTION

Also not helpful? When you are stuck in a perfectionistic mindset, you might procrastinate. A lot. You get overwhelmed by even the idea of starting something that your mind says must be perfect. Not surprisingly, a perfectionistic mindset can end up making you avoid and miss important deadlines, assignments, and opportunities. This leads to more self-critical thoughts and results in feelings of sadness, shame, embarrassment and low self-esteem. Then you strive for even more perfection, as an attempt to feel better about yourself. And the whole cycle keeps going! This is how perfectionistic thoughts keep building on each other and contribute to a negative mood.

Perfectionistic mindset —
"I must get 100 on this paper"

⇩

procrastination —
"I am too overwhelmed to even start"

⇩

avoid starting and miss a deadline

⇩

guilt and self—blame — "I need to make sure my next paper is perfect so I don't feel like such a failure."

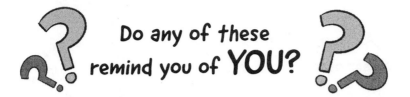

Do any of these remind you of YOU?

- You feel bad about yourself when you don't get the exact grade that you wanted.

- You know your exact grade point averages in each class every quarter.

- You typically feel down, anxious, and insecure when you have nothing to do.

- You often choose studying or practicing over other things that might make you happy, like spending time with friends or relaxing.

- You are in more than two advanced classes by your own choice.

- One mistake can completely ruin your day.

- Family members or friends have told you that you are really hard on yourself.

- You feel a sense of competition with your friends in terms of grades, activities, or popularity.

- You are president or captain of more than two sports teams or clubs.

- You participate in 5 extracurricular activities, maintain a 4.0 GPA, and have no down-time.

Those are typical signs pointing to perfectionism. If you notice more than 4 that fit you, chances are, a perfectionistic mindset may be a source of negative mood for you.

Another place you might spot perfectionism is in your self-talk. Take a look at the list below and count how many statements sound fully or mostly true to you.

- I should do my best 100% of the time, no excuses.
- If I don't make this team, I am a total loser.
- If I'm not first, I'm the first loser.
- I must take the most challenging classes to get into the school I want.
- There are only three colleges that would make me happy.
- People who make mistakes are just careless and need to work harder.
- I need to be in as many AP classes as my smartest friends.
- Other people should always respond quickly when I reach out to them.
- I refuse to lose this debate.
- Being "good enough" is ok for other people, just not for me.

If more than 5 statements above feel mostly true to you, your perfectionistic thoughts are likely keeping you stuck.

Many people confuse **WHAT THEY DO WITH WHO THEY ARE**; when your identity is defined by your accomplishments, your daily mood and self-confidence become dependent on those accomplishments and on how productive you are.

YOU AS A PERSON, BEFORE ANY ACCOMPLISHMENTS, ARE VALUABLE, SPECIAL, AND DESERVING.

By shifting away from perfectionistic thoughts and trying on a more flexible thinking style, you make more room for the deep self-love and acceptance you've been looking for. Not only will you feel happier more often, your success in the areas that are important to you may very well improve.

It is not easy letting go of a perfectionistic mindset. Falling into these thoughts has likely helped you in some ways. At times, perfectionistic thoughts have driven you to work harder, finish your work, and improve your abilities in sports, music, or art. Being seen as a perfectionist may even feel like a part of who you are. The question to ask yourself is: **"AT WHAT COST?"**

Grab a Pen!

Let's do an experiment. Draw a line down the center of a sheet of paper and make a numbered list on each side from 1-10. On one side, come up with 10 ways that holding on to a perfectionistic mindset has helped you. One the other side, write down 10 ways that holding on to a perfectionistic thinking style has hurt you. What have you missed out on? Has it gotten in the way of friendships? Has it made you feel bad about yourself? I'm not rooting for any particular outcome. Try to be as objective as possible and look at the information as data.

What did you learn in that exercise? If you decide that you want to shift away from perfectionistic thinking even just a little bit, the next part of the chapter will have some strategies to get you started.

How do I shift a perfectionistic mindset?

There are two things to do if you want to shake up rigid perfectionistic thinking. First, notice perfectionistic thoughts as they are happening and work on shifting into more flexible thinking and a wider view of yourself. Second, develop a more stable sense of self-worth, a confidence that comes from who you are instead of just what you do or look like on the outside. You will make a big dent in both of these areas by reading and completing the next exercises.

CHALLENGE YOUR PERFECTIONISTIC THOUGHTS

Let's revisit the perfectionistic statements from earlier in the chapter, and practice challenging them. Again, you aren't trying to erase the perfectionistic thoughts, you are just adding additional, more helpful thoughts to the repertoire.

The questions to ask yourself if you get stuck are:

- "What is a more reasonable thought?
- "What is a more helpful thought?"
- "What would my most relaxed and flexible friend be saying?"

PERFECTIONISTIC THINKING	COULD BE TWEAKED LIKE THIS...
I have to get it right, 100% of the time, no excuses.	If I do my best at least one time each day, I have won.
If I don't make this travel team, I am a total loser.	It is ok to not be the very best at every single thing every time.
If you aren't first, you are the first loser.	I almost made it to the final round! I can't believe how tough that was.
I must take the most challenging classes to get into the school I want.	There are many good schools. I have a lot more to offer than just my grades.
There are only three colleges that would make me happy.	Hey, I'm just in middle school! But there are so many colleges that would be great for me.
People who make mistakes are just careless and need to work harder.	Everyone makes mistakes! I bet they are relaxed and happy without the pressure of being perfect.
I need to be in as many AP classes as my smartest friends.	What works for them might not work for me! I need to do what is right for me.
Other people should always respond quickly when I reach out to them.	Everyone is busy! Some of my friends are better than others at paying attention to their phone.
Being "good enough" is ok for other people, just not for me.	Even I know this thought isn't quite fair.

CREATING MORE SELF-LOVE AND TRUE CONFIDENCE

There can't be a book about mood and chapters about thoughts and mindset without talking about inner confidence and self-love. Perfectionistic thinking does not lead to this type of lasting positive relationship with yourself. Again, your sense of your worth is not something you are born with, it is learned. This means that if you struggle with maintaining inner confidence, you can improve how you feel about yourself by learning to shift the way you think about what makes you valuable.

YOU CAN GAIN CONFIDENCE BY CHANGING WHAT YOU SEE AS MOST VALUABLE ABOUT YOU.

To help you develop the type of confidence that is unshakable, unstoppable, and solid, no matter if you are up or down, in a small body or large body, getting good grades or failing grades, struggling with issues around your sexual orientation or gender, getting bullied or being stuck in the role of a bully, surrounded by supportive friends and family or, well…not, winning games or on a losing streak, whether you have a disability or not or are healthy or sick, captain of the team or on the bench for the season, popular or an outcast...here are three tried and true steps to developing true inner confidence (hint...they don't include trying to be perfect):

1. Know the difference between external sources of self-worth and internal sources of self-worth.

2. Identify and intentionally notice inner sources of self-worth.

3. Practice positive self-talk until it feels natural to you.

KNOW THE DIFFERENCE BETWEEN EXTERNAL AND INTERNAL SOURCES OF SELF-WORTH.

What exactly is **externally focused self-worth?** This type of confidence comes from things that we do, achieve, or perform, and often requires a concrete external sign of success such as a grade, a score, a win, a number on the scale, or a compliment from someone. It's something considered valuable outside of you, like scoring the game-winning goal or not missing a single definition on your vocab test.

When you base your sense of self-worth on these outside achievements, your confidence only lasts for a short period of time. Life is not stable, it is unpredictable, full of obstacles, and sprinkled with just enough people who are better, smarter, more popular, and more talented than you to make just about anyone feel insecure.

As long as you are relying on external achievements or others' opinions of you to fill you with inner confidence, you will always run out of those self-loving feelings and you will constantly need to seek more to fill your self-worth tank. You'll end up chasing your sense of worth by external achievement after external achievement after external achievement in order to keep your confidence going.

This is exhausting! The level of mental and emotional energy that is required to constantly fill the tank is not sustainable. While we are busy focusing on self-worth by external achievements, life, actual life, is passing us by. Chances at meaningful connections, moments of wonder, emotional growth, and deep learning escape and so does your sense of joy and positive stable mood. Pretty awful, right?

Unfortunately, for some people, an externally focused sense of self-worth can appear to be working. Sometimes, external achievements satisfy our feelings of self-esteem often enough that our overall confidence feels strong most of the time. On the surface, a person in this fake positive self-esteem cycle can look almost untouchable and like they have it all: confidence, success, friends, popularity, self-love. That is, until a moment when they don't! And that can happen when they don't have anything to do, accomplish, achieve, or perform and no one is around them (like winter break, summer, or even just a weekend of alone time) to notice. This is where an externally focused sense of self-worth reveals its weakness. Instead of feeling a sense of inner calm, peace, and love, chasing externally focused self-worth creates a storm of inner fear, doubt, shame, and a sense of emptiness.

Internally focused self-worth means noticing and holding onto the inner positive qualities that are always inside of us. Instead of focusing on what we *do*, we focus on who we *are*. Instead of focusing on the goal we have met, we are focusing on the inner qualities that allowed us to get there. Instead of looking at the outcome, we look at the process. **IT'S NOT ABOUT THE DESTINATION, IT'S ABOUT THE JOURNEY.** We are often better at noticing internal strengths and value in others than we are in ourselves.

Take a Minute!

Think of someone you really care about. Why do you love them? It's likely that you feel connected to them because of their inner qualities ...not their accomplishments.

External Focus

Let's practice figuring out what internally or externally focused ideas of self-worth look like. Read the following list and think: is this a thought measuring self-worth as an externally focused achievement? Or is it internally focused? In other words, is it about what you do? Or is it about who you are?

1. Where I end up going to college will be the most important thing about me.

2. I feel good because I got into AP English.

3. I am proud of myself for scoring a goal.

4. I'm happy with the way I handled myself when under pressure.

5. I feel good about the way I kept pushing myself even when I knew the game was a lost cause.

6. I am proud of myself for working so hard this year.

7. I love my outfit, even though my friends teased me about it.

8. This year was worth it because I got straight A's.

9. I am proud of myself for applying to be a peer counselor, even though I didn't get the position.

10. I am going to choose an easier class, because I know I deserve to spend more time with my friends.

11. The only way I will be proud of myself is if I win student body president.

12. I don't feel confident about the way I look, because no one complimented me today.

Answer key:

External focus: 1, 2, 3, 8, 11, 12

Internal focus: 4, 5, 6, 7, 9, 10.

Take a Minute!

After reading those examples, think for a minute. Do you ever say things like that to yourself? What was it like for you to read the list?

So how do you know if you are basing your self-worth too much on external sources? Take this quiz to find out!

Take a look at this list and notice which statements you feel strongly represent your mindset when it comes to your self-worth.

- I care a lot about other people's opinions of me.

- The way I feel about myself is tied to what other people think about how I look.

- I feel really bad about myself when I am not better than those around me at something.

- When my grades are As, I feel good about myself, but my self-esteem plummets if I get a B or C.

- When my parents are mad at me, I feel like a bad person and my emotions fall apart.

- My self-esteem is strongly tied to always doing exactly the right thing.

How strongly do you believe the statements above? How many "feel" fully true to you? How often do thoughts like this come up for you? What percentage of your life, time, energy, and thoughts is occupied by fear, stress, or negative mood around these issues? The answers to these questions will give you some information about where your sense of confidence comes from (outside of you or from within).

IDENTIFY AND INTENTIONALLY NOTICE INNER SOURCES OF SELF-WORTH.

First, let's help you identify your positive internal qualities, so that you know what to focus on. As you complete the following sections, think about the inner qualities that make you who you are.

What do you like about yourself? What has helped you get through tough times in your life? What strengths do you see in yourself when no one is watching? Who are you when no one is around to see it?

Grab a Pen! ✒️

Jot these down on a piece of paper or make a note in your phone as you answer each question. Or just take a minute to answer them to yourself.

1. What are 3 things that you appreciate about who you are that have nothing to do with your external achievements or something you have "done?" Think about your characteristics or parts of your personality that you value.

2. What is something you really like about yourself that most people in your life don't know about?

3. What would a close friend say about you if I asked them what they love about you? (Chances are they would not say "she gets As all the time," or "he is the best-looking person in our class.")

4. If I asked one of your parents what three things are most valuable about you, what would they say? They probably wouldn't say "he scores a goal in every game." The next time you see one of your parents, ask them that question. You might just be surprised by the answer.

5. What do you see as your greatest inner strengths? Write them down.

NOW THAT YOU HAVE A WHOLE LIST OF STRENGTHS IN FRONT OF YOU, YOU'RE SEEING YOURSELF IN A NEW LIGHT, RIGHT?

Now it's time to take your confidence to the next level by **INTENTIONALLY NOTICING** these strengths on a daily basis. Think of the last external achievement you felt good about. Now come up with three internal qualities that helped you achieve that goal. Feeling stuck? Check out the examples below to give you some ideas.

EXTERNAL ACHIEVEMENT: We won the soccer game and I scored a goal.
INTERNAL QUALITIES: I worked hard all summer to improve my skills, I'm dedicated and passionate.

EXTERNAL ACHIEVEMENT: We got an A on a group project.
INTERNAL QUALITIES: I am a good leader, I connected well with my partners, I didn't quit when things got hard.

External achievements are what you *do* and internal qualities are who you *are*. The trick is to make sure to recognize the amazing things about you that helped you get to your goal. What is it about you, your values, and your journey that helped you succeed? Those are your internal strengths!

PRACTICE POSITIVE SELF-TALK UNTIL IT FEELS NATURAL TO YOU.

Now that you've learned the difference between internal and external sources of self-worth, opened your eyes to your inner strengths, and practiced intentionally noticing them, you can move on to the last step!

Time to work on self-talk and continue to grow some new brain pathways. Words can be incredibly powerful, and by practicing speaking to yourself differently, you can grow that inner, bright, deep confidence that I've been talking about.

Grab a Pen!

Below are some of my favorite positive self-talk statements. Pick out four or five that resonate with you, save them in your notebook or phone, and read them every day. Add to the list whenever you feel inspired.

- ☐ I know who I am, and I am enough.
- ☐ It's ok to have weaknesses, and it's ok to accept them. I have to hold both my strengths and my weaknesses at the same time, and everyone has both.
- ☐ I am grateful for what I have.
- ☐ I am not what I do.
- ☐ I have value as a human being, just by existing, living, and breathing.
- ☐ There will always be someone who doesn't like me and that's ok.
- ☐ What my body looks like is the least interesting thing about me.
- ☐ I have more to offer the world than what people see on the outside.
- ☐ I am choosing to embrace my strengths.
- ☐ I love challenges and what I learn by overcoming them.
- ☐ I can do things that are hard.

Take-Away!

Unlike what you may have assumed, a perfectionistic thinking style (like other thinking mistakes) is not always helpful or positive. While it can be helpful in some ways, it has some major downsides, including negative mood, feelings of emptiness, and low feelings of self-worth in the long term. The most valuable characteristics associated with success, productivity, and joy are actually **FLEXIBILITY, GRIT, AND INNER CONFIDENCE.**

What kind of confidence leads to a positive mood and deep well-being?

The kind that is based on our inner values and character. What we do when no-one is watching, and there is no external reward, is more important to focus on than our external achievements like grades, scores, and wins. Focusing inward and basing your confidence on who you are instead of what you achieve or do is the path to more happiness, true confidence, a positive mood, and unshakable self-esteem.

chapter 9

Actions Are Superpowers

$\mathcal{I}$n this chapter, you will learn about the part of the mood cycle that gives you the most bang for your buck when it comes to improving your mood. Listening to your body, shifting your thoughts and mindset, and managing your emotions are all very important, but without taking positive actions, the whole positive mood cycle falls apart. It's all about just doing it...

IT ALL COMES DOWN TO THE ACTIONS YOU TAKE.

In general, there are **UP actions** that help create a positive mood and **DOWN actions** that keep us stuck in a negative mood. Importantly, most people think they should wait until they feel better or more ready before taking UP actions, but this doesn't really work! You're waiting until you already feel better before you try to feel better...how does that make sense? All you need is a **willingness** to take the chance and take charge of your wellbeing by choosing to do daily habits (even small ones) that will help create a positive mood. Easier said than done, I know!

Some of these UP actions will be those that we know are likely to improve mood for most people, and others will be based on your own **personal values** (actions that matter most to you).

THE SMALL ACTIONS YOU CHOOSE ON A DAILY BASIS ARE YOUR SUPERPOWER.

Take a Minute!

What are some choices and habits that you wish you put more energy into? Keep these in your mind as you read the chapter, set an intention, and write them down on paper!

When you take UP actions that bring you either a sense of **JOY** or **ACCOMPLISHMENT**, you'll notice feeling better right away (at least for a little while) because right away your brain will produce mood-improving neurochemicals (remember Chapter 3?). Over time, your brain begins to connect these actions to a positive emotion, and you'll end up actually *wanting* to take UP actions more often. The more you continue to take UP actions, the more likely you are to find yourself in situations that help improve your mood in the long term. The more often you engage in UP actions, even when you don't feel like it, the greater your chance of having a positive emotional experience. In this way, UP actions build on each other and keep a positive mood going.

Now, taking one of these UP actions *one time* won't magically make you feel amazing. Instead, it's choosing to take UP actions on a regular, consistent basis that leads to feeling great.

TAKING UP ACTIONS GETS EASIER OVER TIME.

UP ACTIONS

Researchers have discovered that the UP actions most associated with a positive mood include activities related to nutrition, sleep, movement, social connection, being outdoors, helping others, and meditating. Here are some general recommendations so you know what to aim for:

NUTRITION

Fueling your body in a way that feels nourishing and energy-promoting is key to a balanced mood. Think of food as energizing and restorative! Be mindful of how different eating patterns and foods make your body feel, and make sure to get enough nutrients to support the activities you are asking of your body.

Some general guidelines to aim for: eat a wide variety of fruits and vegetables, eat balanced meals (each meal or snack should have a serving of fat, protein, and fiber), include foods that you enjoy and that leave you feeling satisfied. Check out the examples for more details about what your plate could look like, and how to get a wide variety of foods from all the major food groups.

One thing to note: You are probably not buying your own groceries and don't have control over the food you get at school. In fact, most kids don't really have a choice in what food ends up on their table! So do the best you can when you can.

HEALTHY OILS

WATER

VEGETABLES

WHOLE GRAINS

FRUITS

HEALTHY PROTEIN

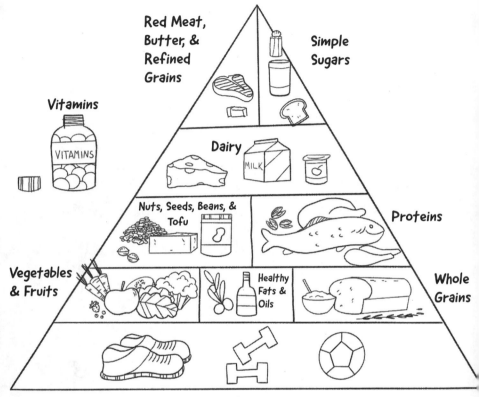

SLEEP

The recommended amount of sleep that is ideal for a balanced mood at your age is at least nine hours a night. Sleep experts recommend waking up and going to bed at the same time every day (even weekends should be within one to two hours of your typical wake up and bedtimes). Practicing calm breathing, stopping screen use for at least an hour before bed, and using another self-soothing strategy (remember Chapter 4?) around bedtime can help set you up for success.

MOVEMENT

Anything counts when it comes to physical exercise, and any movement is better than no movement at all. Try to move your body in a way that brings you joy or accomplishment every single day. You can start small and take a 15 minute walk each day, eventually working up to an hour of movement a day. Pay attention to how you feel during and after the activity, and how you talk to yourself. If you approach this task as a daily part of your life, it will get easier with time. If exercise is not a part of your life right now, take small concrete steps and focus on the journey instead of the result. Meet your body where it is today and intentionally find gratitude for what your body *can* do instead of what it *can't*.

SOCIAL CONNECTION

Try to reach out to at least one friend and connect with at least one family member each day. The goal is to put energy and effort into our relationships in order for them to feel rewarding and close. Spending time with people we care about, even in small ways and for a short time, is key. Think: *quality over quantity*. It's more important to have true friends and meaningful connections, not necessarily many of them.

HELPING OTHERS

Giving support to and helping others can be many different things. Try to look for opportunities such as: listening when someone is in need, offering to talk, reaching out to someone who is struggling, smiling at a stranger, defending the underdog, giving a compliment, or doing community service.

GETTING OUTSIDE

Spending time outdoors, even if you live in a city, can have a big impact on your mood. Getting fresh air can be so grounding. Work towards going outside during daylight every single day, even if it is only for a few minutes. Bonus points if you combine movement (walking or yoga) with getting outdoors. Overachiever? Studies have shown that 20 minutes a day of being outdoors creates significant positive mood shifts.

MEDITATING

Meditating clears our mind, calms us down, improves our mood in the moment, and makes us happier in the long-term (I am not kidding about how powerful it can be). Any amount is better than none at all, but most experts agree that 20 minutes a day is the sweet spot. There are many ways to meditate, and many accessible apps to get you started. Some of our favorites include Calm, Insight Timer, and Headspace.

TAKING SMALL UP ACTIONS ON A REGULAR BASIS IS YOUR TICKET TO A GOOD MOOD.

PRO TIP

I know I told you to limit excessive screen use (you caught me!). So if using these apps before bed, set your phone on do not disturb, lower the brightness, and try to just listen to the sound instead of watching the screen.

DOWN ACTIONS

One way to increase the number of UP actions you are regularly taking is to decrease the number of DOWN actions.

Some common DOWN actions that are tied to a negative mood include:

- Staying up too late
- Being inactive, lying around: not moving enough

- Not getting enough nutrients (eating non-nutritious food, eating too much or not eating enough)

- Isolating from others (not reaching out, not returning texts)

- Spending too much time on screens and on social media

- Staying indoors and not getting enough time outside

- Procrastinating on schoolwork or straight-up not doing it

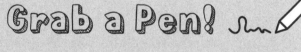

Grab a Pen!

Ready to take charge of your mood? Write down two to three UP action categories that you think could use improvement and set a small, specific, and doable goal to aim for each week. Example: I will go to bed at 10pm at least four days this week. Next week, I will go for two 30-minute walks outside.

PERSONAL VALUES

Now, I know you are your own person, and you may already be thinking of some UP actions and DOWN actions that you engage in that I haven't listed. What are you doing when you feel your best? What are you typically doing when you feel your worst?

The way to get the most out of taking UP actions is to focus on actions that are aligned with your personal values. Your personal values are what YOU find most meaningful and important in YOUR life. They define **WHO YOU ARE, HOW YOU TREAT OTHERS, AND WHAT YOU VALUE THE MOST.** Sometimes your personal values may go against what is cool or exciting to those around you. When this happens, it can be challenging to know which action to choose. Just remember, UP actions that are most consistent with your own personal values will be the biggest mood-boosters by far.

FOCUSING ON YOUR OWN PERSONAL VALUES WHEN MAKING CHOICES IS THE BIGGEST MOOD BOOSTER.

You may know what some of your personal values are already, but in case you need some inspiration, here are some common ones.

Excellence   GROWTH

HONESTY   RULES   Loyalty   Integrity

Quality   Trust   Competence

SERVICE   Achievement   Ethics

Family   Innovation

Faith   Conduct   Collaboration

Accountability   PERSONAL GROWTH

CONSISTENCY   ORGANIZATION

Commitment   Correctness   SCHOOL LiFE BALANCE

TEAMWORK

JUSTICE   OPENNESS

Friendship   NATURE

Take a Minute!

Which five personal values feel most relevant to who you are or who you want to be? Grab a pen and write them down. Keep them somewhere easily accessible so you can use them as a compass the next time you are choosing to take or not take an action.

YOUR PERSONAL VALUES ARE WHAT YOU FIND MOST MEANINGFUL AND IMPORTANT IN YOUR LIFE.

SUPER-CHARGE YOUR UP ACTIONS

Now that you have a sense of the actions that are most important to put your energy into, let's take a look at some tips to live by as you get started. Before you know it, taking UP actions will become a habit and feel so much easier.

Here are five tips to SUPER-CHARGE your UP ACTIONS:

ACTION before MOTIVATION

Write It Down!

Here – Now
—— instead of ——
When – Then

Countdown
5, 4, 3, 2, 1

Start Small

Once you start to use these strategies, you will feel more in control, confident, and empowered to take your mood to the next level. A few new habits can make a big impact on your life!

ACTION BEFORE MOTIVATION

Do you ever hear your mind saying "It's just too hard," "I don't have time," "I don't really want to," "It takes too much effort," or "I'll start when school is over, when it's nice outside, when the season is over, when exams are over, or when I feel better..."?

My brain is guilty of producing these thoughts too! The problem is, you won't actually *want* to do these things until you start doing them and see some positive results. The solution? **JUST DO IT!** That's right. You have to actually do the things that might make you feel better over time before you feel motivated to do them.

IT IS NOT ABOUT *WANTING* TO TAKE ACTION, IT IS ABOUT BEING *WILLING* TO TRY.

A Call to Action:

Grab a pen and paper and write down one UP action that you are willing to take TODAY.

A HERE–NOW MENTALITY

Just like "action before motivation," instead of waiting for the When...Then, take action Right Here, Right Now! This tip helps us focus on the present moment, instead of waiting for "someday" in the future and some perfect situation. Some questions to help guide you to make choices for yourself in the Here–Now include:

- Which part of this can I do **RIGHT NOW?**
- What is the first step that I can take **TODAY?**
- Is there any piece of this that I can move toward **THIS VERY MOMENT?**
- What is the **NEXT** UP action I can take?

When–Then Mindset

Here are some examples of a When–Then mindset vs. a Here–Now mindset. Can you tell which is which?

I'll only invite my friend over once they invite me first. It's too awkward.

I'm going to text my friend right now, even if it's not to ask her to come over yet. At least it's a starting point.

I'm going to try out for the lacrosse team once I improve my running speed.

I am going to try out now, because I know I want to play (even if I'm not sure I'll make it).

I'll run for student council my senior year, once I know more people in my class.

I am going to get involved no matter what, and if I don't make it far, at least I'll get some practice for next year.

I am going to start exercising once summer starts and I have more time.

I'm really busy, but I am going to fit in a 15-minute yoga routine every morning starting today.

I will raise my hand in class once I feel confident that I know the answer.

I need to raise my hand now, even if I'm not sure of the answer. I can handle it if I don't get it right.

I am going to try to score a goal once I get the perfect pass and am sure I can do it.

I won't ever score if I don't ever try. Like – right – now.

I will ask for a classmate's phone number after a few more weeks of school, when I feel more comfortable.

I don't feel confident enough now, but I know conection is a personal value of mine, so here I go!

I'll take a dance class once I feel better about my body.

I'm going to take a beginner dance class today. I can focus on feeling better instead of looking at my body.

I'll start my schoolwork after the next TV show.

I am going to do my first assignment now, and work on it for just 10 minutes.

I'll tell my friends about how upset I've been feeling, but only after they ask me if I'm ok.

I may not feel brave enough to confide in my friends fully, but I do think I can ask them if we can schedule a time to talk.

WRITE IT DOWN!

Did you know that people who write down their goal and keep track of their progress (called "self-monitoring) instead of just keeping it in their mind are 50% more likely to achieve that goal? This is seriously weird, but true.

So give it a try. Set an intention to take one UP action per day and write it down! Another strategy that can help? Imagine yourself taking that action, focus on images of yourself making that choice, and get in touch with how it would feel.

COUNT DOWN 5, 4, 3, 2, 1

When you want to take an UP action but just can't seem to take the first step, count down in your mind or out loud from five to one. The key to using this strategy lies in quickly taking an UP action before you have a chance to think twice about it. It's sort of like a runner at the start of a race; you can't hesitate, even for a second, or you will be left behind.

START SMALL

Setting your sights too high at the beginning can set you up for failure. The most important thing at the early stage of learning new habits is to follow through so you can gain confidence. You are better off starting with a very small UP action that you are fully confident you can get done. This way, you make room for gratitude, pride, and a sense of accomplishment that keeps you motivated to do more and more.

Casey, when their mood was at its worst, was having a tough time getting out of bed in the morning. They were going to sleep late at night, after scrolling through social media on their phone for hours. This never really felt comforting, and most of the time actually left them feeling sad and lonely. Over the summer, making plans with friends felt like too much effort. They chose not to go to camp as they felt anxious being around new people. All in all, Casey did not feel like doing much of anything, and their mindset was "things will feel easier when school starts again."

So with a bit of a nudge, Casey worked really hard to implement more UP actions using some of the strategies in this chapter. Not only did they feel better in the short term, they also re-learned that they have close friends in their life that reliably help them feel supported and loved.

Here are some strategies that Casey found helpful:

Sleep: Casey set an alarm for each night to remind them of their goal of going to bed earlier. They reminded themselves that feeling less exhausted in the daytime was important to living consistently with one of their personal values: growth and excellence. Casey also achieved their goal of waking up at the same time every morning. They used the 5, 4, 3, 2, 1 strategy to help themselves literally jump out of bed as soon as their alarm went off. Casey would lay in bed, hear the alarm, and tell themselves "in five seconds I will put my feet on the floor, 5...4...3...2...1 GO!"

Movement and getting outdoors: Walking outside was hard for Casey, even though they immediately felt a more positive mood after beginning their walking routine. It was hot outside, and they never felt motivated to go. Casey reminded themselves of the "action before motivation" strategy, which they wrote down in their phone and looked at daily.

Connection: Casey was feeling worried and nervous about calling their debate team partner. They kept falling into a when–then mindset ("when I feel more energy, then I will call him"). What helped the most was shifting to a here–now mindset by asking themselves which part of the goal they could achieve on that particular day. The answer? They ended up texting instead of calling; this felt like a smaller and easier step to accomplish.

Take-Away!

In this chapter, you learned that a great deal of your power in terms of your mood lies in choosing to take positive UP actions more often and decreasing the frequency of DOWN actions.

Taking UP actions that are in line with your own personal values will boost your mood most powerfully. Other UP actions that are likely to improve your mood in the short and long term include activities that support:

- Helping others
- Social connections
- Sleep
- Movement
- Nutrition
- Getting outside
- Meditation

Do you remember the intention you set at the start of the chapter? Which area above do you want to put more energy into? What do you want this to look like? Make a choice and use the strategies you learned in this chapter (action before motivation, choosing to act in the here and now, writing it down, counting back from 5 to 1, and starting small) to help get you there.

I KNOW THAT YOU HAVE EVERYTHING IT TAKES TO SUCCEED ALREADY INSIDE OF YOU, SO ARE YOU WILLING?

Chapter 10

If Things Are Too Much (How to Ask for Help)

$\mathcal{T}$ his chapter is dedicated to all of the kids who have faced challenges, struggles, and stressors that are invisible to others on the outside. I hope that you no longer feel alone. Give yourself permission to dream of your future, achieve inner peace, and create the relationship with yourself that you deserve to have. You are lovable, capable, and have all of the ingredients to create a life full of well-being and peace already within you. **IT IS WHO YOU ARE.**

WELCOME TO THE LAST CHAPTER OF THIS BOOK!

Now, the last stop on your journey here includes learning how to manage moments when a negative emotion becomes very intense and takes over. This is called "emotional flooding." Have you ever had a moment where you were feeling an emotion, like anger or sadness, so powerfully that you couldn't even think straight? It feels hard to even notice what it feels like in your body, because things go from 0-100 in a few short seconds. In this chapter, you will learn exactly what to do in these moments, so that you can get to your baseline more quickly, and without reacting in a way that you might later regret.

If you have ever felt helpless about your mood or life's challenges, and have wanted to gain the courage to ask for help, this chapter will guide you on how to do that! I'll go over mental health issues like depression, and red flags that may tell you it is time to take action and talk to a trusted adult. Even more importantly, you will get lots of ideas about how exactly to tell someone how you feel and have these important conversations in a way that feels meaningful to you.

And if you are curious about therapy or other treatment options for challenges related to your mood, I've got you covered at the end of this chapter. I'll talk about how to find a therapist, knowing what different types of therapy are offered, and give you the scoop on common medication options.

EMOTIONAL FLOODING

Have you ever had a moment of such intense emotion in your body that you feel like you are going to explode? Have you ever acted in a way that afterwards felt completely irrational and confusing to you? Have you ever seen someone totally lose control of their emotions and say things or do things that are out of character for them? This is emotional flooding, and it is one of the most uncomfortable experiences that we can have. The bad news is, there is quite literally nothing you can do to avoid flooding once it starts, or make flooding instantly stop. The good news is, you are in control of how you respond in that situation, and can choose to take care of yourself emotionally and physically so that you don't end up doing or saying something you regret.

IT IS YOUR BRAIN (AGAIN)!

Imagine you are taking a walk in the woods in the dark. You are certain that you just heard a noise in the bushes, and it sounds like something large. Immediately your heart starts racing, your ears may throb as they try to hear any noise, your body tenses up in preparation to run at the speed of light away from a bear, and you feel heat rising through your legs and chest. That feeling? That is your brain doing its job to try to save your life in the face of a threat. Flashback! Flooding is like a bigger version of what you have already learned about in Chapter 3; the feeling brain is intensely activated, so much so that the volume on the thinking brain is turned way down. This makes perfect sense *if* we are actually running from a bear. We don't have time to think, and in order to survive we have to run as fast as possible. If we stopped in that moment and thought to ourselves, "hmm I wonder if I should run or if I should try to play dead instead?" well, you can imagine what would happen.

 FLOODING = SUPER ACTIVATED FEELING BRAIN AND DEACTIVATED THINKING BRAIN.

So how can you respond differently?

There are several action steps that you can take to get yourself out of the sticky mess of flooding. Your goal is to give your body enough time away from the threat so your feeling brain can start to calm down and the thinking brain can turn up again. Then you are in a much better position to get your balance back and make choices that are consistent with who you want to be or who you are at your best.

1. Recognize the first signs of flooding in your body and GET OUT OR AWAY. Here are some common signs:

- Trouble focusing, like your brain is trying to process a lot of info at once
- Suddenly feeling afraid or withdrawing mentally
- Feeling like your brain is overheating or turning off
- Everything feels dangerous, bad, or wrong
- Feeling unsafe even when nothing around you is physically threatening
- Feeling your emotions all over the place and not being able to pinpoint them
- Physical symptoms like sweaty hands, tunnel vision, lightheadedness, knot in stomach, increased heart rate and blood pressure, quick & shallow breathing, tightness in jaw

Take a Minute!

Do you know what your body does when you start to get overwhelmed?

2. Wait at least 20 minutes before returning to the situation. I did not make that number up. It's science!

Fun Fact:

When your body is responding to what it thinks is a threat to your life, your "feeling brain" sends a signal to your adrenal glands to quickly and intensely release stress hormones (adrenaline and cortisol) to the body, which creates the "fight, flight, freeze" response. Once released, these hormones take 20 minutes cycle through the body before your heart rate returns to normal.

3. While you are waiting for your body to naturally return to balance, practice strategies to:

- relax your body: calm breathing, hands on heart or belly

- steady your thinking: be prepared with helpful self-talk

- make a plan of action: what is the wisest way to respond?

Remember Jacob? Well, he had a predictable trigger of flooding that got his body headed towards an explosion of emotion on an almost weekly basis: his older brother Tom. Every time Tom had friends over, he would make comments out loud in front of his friends about Jacob that were embarrassing.

One day, Tom and his friends casually strolled by the room Jacob was studying in and Tom said: "no wonder you sucked so badly in the game yesterday, you'll never get better with your nose in a book all the time." Just the sound of Tom's voice had the power to get Jacob's emotional system revved up. He felt like he wanted to scream! He felt humiliated and enraged at the same time!

Do you remember a time when your body flooded with emotion? What did you do? What do you wish you had done? What did you do right?

Normally, Jacob would have done something like running up to Tom and pushing him, getting into a screaming match, or throwing something he actually cared about, like his phone. But he knew he needed to practice responding differently to his emotions, so this time he went through these steps to try to untangle himself from his usual pattern:

1. Jacob noticed the first signs of flooding: his body always started building heat in his chest and arms. Immediately, Jacob left his room and went outside to sit on the deck to get away from Tom.

2. Jacob was tempted to go back inside and give Tom a piece of his mind, but he tried his best to stay outside for 20 whole minutes.

3. By minute 20, Jacob felt more relaxed, and began practicing calm breathing for another five

minutes. Deep breaths in, deep breaths out. Once he was calm, Jacob asked himself what the wisest choice was in this situation, and realized just ignoring the whole situation would be best.

4. Last, but not least, Jacob was already armed with several self-talk thoughts that he created ahead of time and saved in his phone. The ones that resonated the most in that moment included:

- I can take control of my body to take control of my choices.
- If I respond to Tom, I'm giving him exactly what he wants.
- If I give myself time and space, I win and Tom loses.
- I get to decide how I want to respond.
- It takes my body 20 minutes to calm down, I need to give it a chance.
- Yes I'm flooded, but I'm safe and I'll feel better in a few minutes.

Jacob worked on defining his idea of success in this situation based on his own value system. He valued personal agency wanted to feel in control of his responses, so staying cool was huge.

Take a Minute!

Can you practice taking these three steps the next time you notice your body starting to overflow with emotion?

COULD YOU HAVE DEPRESSION?

You already learned how we think about and tease apart typical mood swings from something more serious like depression in Chapter 2. Remember severity, duration, and areas of impact? Let's improve your ability to spot when you need to ask for help, for yourself or even for a friend. Here you will learn about common signs of depression and bipolar depression, along with some "code red" signs that should be paid attention to immediately by talking to a trusted adult, calling a helpline, or even calling 9-1-1.

CODE RED = talk to a trusted adult ASAP

Depression is a mental health illness that interferes with your ability to handle your daily life including sleep, eating, school, and social life. Unlike more typical mood shifts, it is more intense or long-lasting. **DEPRESSION IS IN NO WAY A SIGN OF WEAKNESS OR A CHARACTER FLAW.** Many things underlie depression including your genes, environment, and brain chemistry, and most people need treatment to get better. Know that you're not alone; 13.3% of U.S. teens between the ages of 12-17 have at least one episode of depression. If you think you might be struggling with depression, here are some questions to help you get clear:

- Do I constantly feel sad, anxious, or even "empty," like I feel nothing?
- Do I feel hopeless or like everything is going wrong?
- Do I feel like I'm worthless or helpless?
- Do I feel guilty about things?
- Do I feel irritable a lot of the time?
- Do I spend more time alone and push my friends and family away?

- Are my grades dropping?
- Have I lost interest or joy in activities that I used to like doing?
- Am I eating or sleeping more or less than usual?
- Do I always feel tired? Like I have less energy than normal or no energy at all?
- Do I feel restless and have trouble sitting still?
- Do I have a hard time focusing, remembering information, or making decisions?
- Do I have aches or pains, headaches, cramps, or stomach problems that don't have a clear cause?
- Do I think about dying or suicide? Have I ever tried to harm myself?

Take a Minute!

What was reading that list like? Not everyone with depression has all of these symptoms or feels them all of the time, and how long they last varies from person to person.

Bipolar depression is a mental health disease that causes unusual shifts in mood, energy, activity levels, and day-to-day functioning. It can include all of the signs of depression along with additional symptoms:

- Noticeable, and sometimes extreme changes in mood and behavior that are very different than usual.

- Racing thoughts and trouble staying focused.

- Having trouble sleeping but not feeling tired.

- Having a short temper and feeling extremely irritable.

- Engaging in risky or reckless behavior that isn't typical.

- A plan or intention of suicide.

- Writing a goodbye letter.

- Posting about suicide on social media.

- Thinking about death.

- Hearing things that others do not hear (auditory hallucinations).

- Seeing things that others do not see (visual hallucinations).

- Engaging in or thinking about cutting, hitting, biting, or other means of hurting your body.

Suicide is a permanent solution to a temporary problem (remember how quickly emotions can shift?).

THERE IS LITERALLY NOTHING IN LIFE THAT YOU CAN'T TROUBLE-SHOOT, SOLVE, OR USE TO FUEL YOUR SUPERPOWERS.

HOW IS DEPRESSION TREATED?

Although depression is a serious condition, it is treatable. You should get evaluated, diagnosed, and treated by a healthcare provider. This could be your pediatrician, a therapist, or a psychiatrist.

Typically, depression is treated with therapy, medication, or a combination of the two. Cognitive behavioral therapy, or CBT for short, has been shown to be the most effective type of therapy for depression (and anxiety too!). It focuses on helping you shift your body, thoughts, mindset, and actions. Sound familiar? This book is based on principles of CBT. A therapist who uses CBT will help you learn tools and strategies to cope with depression in healthier ways, and help you understand yourself on a deeper level.

Acceptance and commitment therapy (ACT for short) has also been shown to be helpful in these areas and focuses on accepting uncomfortable emotions and living your life based on your inner values. Sound familiar? Yup, I definitely sprinkled some ACT skills in this book too.

Several types of medications can help treat symptoms of depression. Different people respond to medications differently, and you may need to try different types to see which one works best for you. The most common medications prescribed for depression are selective serotonin reuptake inhibitors (SSRIs), and they increase the level of serotonin in the brain, increasing feelings of happiness and well-being. At your age, there is a small chance that certain medications will cause you to feel even worse, so pay attention to how you are feeling and talk to your doctor openly and honestly.

With treatment, you can get better over time, and it is always more effective when you work together with your therapist, physician, and parents as a team. No matter which treatment type you choose, feeling connected to and empowered by your treatment team is key. Feeling better can take time but sticking with your treatment plan can help you manage your symptoms and reduce the likelihood of you experiencing them again in the future.

HOW DO I ASK FOR HELP?

The most important step here is talking to a trusted adult about how you have been feeling—your parent, teacher, school counselor, pastor, mentor, or even a close friend's parent are all good choices. If you don't feel comfortable telling an adult, try talking to a friend.

ASKING FOR HELP IS A SIGN OF MATURITY AND TAKING CARE OF YOURSELF IS SOMETHING TO BE PROUD OF.

To give you some ideas about opening up the conversation, take a look at a few things Casey told their parents:

No. Nothing has happened. It just hit me out of nowhere and I think I've been feeling like this for a while. I think I might have depression.

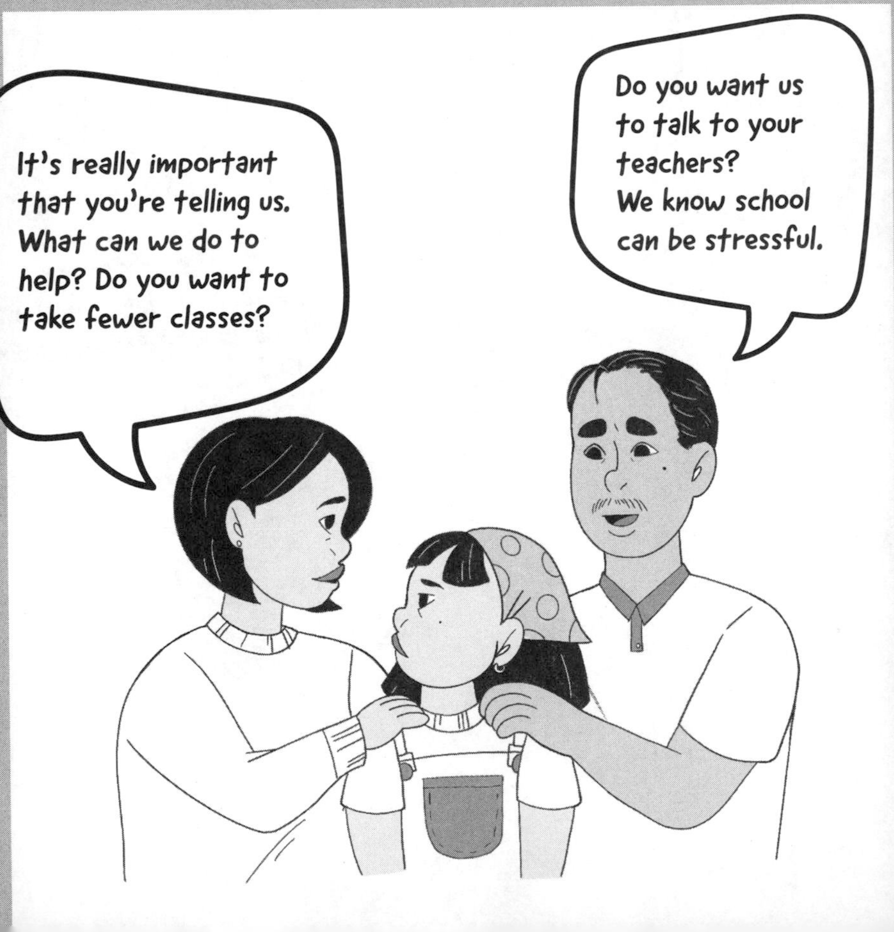
It's really important that you're telling us. What can we do to help? Do you want to take fewer classes?
Do you want us to talk to your teachers? We know school can be stressful.

Take a Minute!

Do you think it would go this well with an adult in your life? What are you most afraid of? What do you think could help you take the step?

HOW DO I HELP A FRIEND?

If you think a friend might have depression, your first step is to help them talk to a trusted adult. There are other things that are also important like:

- Being supportive, patient, and encouraging, even if you don't totally understand what is going on.

- Invite them to activities or just to hang out, **EVEN IF THEY KEEP SAYING NO.**

- Remind them that there are treatments available, and that therapy or medications may not be as scary as they think.

- If you hear them make comments about death, self-harm, or suicide, even if it sounds like they are joking or being dramatic, take it seriously. Talk to a trusted adult as soon as you can, even if it means your friend will be mad at you in the moment. **IT'S JUST NOT WORTH REGRETTING NOT SAYING SOMETHING IF ANYTHING WERE TO HAPPEN.**

If you are worried about being able to keep yourself safe, or hear a friend say they are going to kill themselves (or even make a comment or post on social media that worries you) your best step, in addition to telling an adult, is:

▦ Call 911 and tell them how you are feeling or what you are seeing.

Other options if you are in a crisis and don't know where to turn are:

▦ National Suicide Prevention Lifeline at **1-800-273-TALK**

▦ Crisis Text Line—text **HELLO** to **741741**

 These lines are confidential, free, and open 24/7

Take-Away!

Congratulations! You have made it to your destination on this journey. Your brain connections have grown and expanded immensely since you first opened this book (thanks again, neuroplasticity!). The skills you have learned in shifting your body, thoughts, mindset, emotions, and actions are invaluable, and I just know they will come in handy throughout your life. You have set yourself up for success in navigating not only the mood challenges of middle school, but also the emotional challenges that the universe will inevitably throw your way from time to time in the future. You were already strong, smart, and resilient before this book, but now? Now you are strong, smart, resilient and have ownership over your emotional life. Your superpower? Knowing how to change the things in your life that you can control and being able to face things you have no power over with more ease and acceptance. Armed with a gratitude, self-compassion, and growth mindset, you are literally unstoppable. Now, how do you want to use your superpower today?

Extra Resources

*D*ear readers. I want to share with you some of my favorite books, movies, and websites. I carefully selected this list to include only the resources that I use frequently myself, and that I personally recommend to my clients.

RECOMMENDED BOOKS FOR TWEENS AND TEENS

Alvord, M. K., & McGrath, A. (2017). *Conquer negative thinking for teens: A workbook to break the nine thought habits that are holding you back.* New Harbinger.

Battistin, J. (2019). *Mindfulness for teens in 10 minutes a day.* Rockridge Press.

Brundage, V. (2018). *Shoot your shot: A sport-inspired guide to living your best life.*

Covey, S. (2014). *The 7 habits of highly effective teens.* Touchstone.

Curley, P. (2020). *Growth mindset workbook for kids.* Rockridge Press.

Krimer, K. (2020). *The essential self-compassion workbook for teens: Overcome your inner critic and fully embrace yourself.* Rockridge Press.

Sedley, B. (2017). *Stuff that sucks: A teen's guide to accepting what you can't change and committing to what you can*. Instant Help.

Snel, E. (2013). *Sitting still like a frog: Mindfulness exercises for kids (and their parents)*. Shambhala.

Sperling, J. (2021). *Find your fierce: How to put social anxiety in its place*. Magination Press.

Tompkins, M. A., & Martinez, K. A. (2010). *My anxious mind: A teen's guide to managing anxiety and panic*. Magination Press.

Zucker, B. (2022). *A perfectionist's guide to not being perfect*. Magination Press.

RECOMMENDED BOOKS AND ONLINE SOURCES FOR PARENTS AND ADULT CAREGIVERS

Alvord, M. K., Grados, J. J, & Zucker, B. (2011). *Resilience builder program for children and adolescents: Enhancing social competence and self-regulation*. Research Press.

Clarke-Fields, H., & Naumburg, C. (2019). *Raising good humans: A mindful guide to breaking the cycle of reactive parenting and raising kind, confident kids*. New Harbinger.

Harris, R., & Hayes, S. (2008). *The happiness trap: How to stop struggling and start living: A guide to ACT*. Trumpeter.

Harvey, P., & Penzo, J. (2009). *Parenting a child who has intense emotions: Dialectical behavior therapy skills to help your child regulate emotional outbursts and aggressive behaviors*. New Harbinger.

Lebowitz, E. R. (2021). *Breaking free of childhood anxiety and OCD: A scientifically proven program for parents*. Oxford University Press.

Martin, M. M., & Swinson, R. P. (2009). *When perfect isn't good enough: Strategies for coping with perfectionism*. New Harbinger.

Neff, K. (2015). *Self-compassion: The proven power of being kind to yourself.* William Morrow.

Niequist, S. (2016). *Present over perfect: Leaving behind frantic for a simpler, more soulful way of living.* Zondervan.

Stixrud, W., & Johnson, N. (2019). *The self-driven child: The science and sense of giving your kids more control over their lives.* Penguin Books.

Zucker, B. (2017). *Anxiety-free kids: An interactive guide for parents and children.* Routledge.

VIDEOS AND PODCASTS

Costa, C. (2021, March). *How gratitude rewires your brain* [Video]. Ted Conferences. http://ted.com/talks/christina_costa_how_gratitude_rewires_your_brain

Damour, L. (Host). (2019, May). Anxiety and teen girls (No. 80) [Audio podcast episode]. In *Speaking of Psychology.* American Psychological Association. http:// apa.org/news/podcasts/speaking-of-psychology/anxiety-teen-girls

David, S. (2020, May). *Checking in* [Video]. Ted Conferences. http://ted.com/talks/checking_in_with_susan_david_self_compassion_for_the_self_critical

Gilmartin, P. (Host). (2011–present). *Mental illness happy hour* [Audio podcast]. http://mentalpod.com

Kaiser, R. (2019, October). *Teen brains are not broken* [Video]. Ted Conferences. http://ted.com/talks/roselinde_kaiser_ph_d_teen_brains_are_not_broken

Ricard, M. (2004, February). *The habits of happiness* [Video]. Ted Conferences. http://ted.com/talks/matthieu_ricard_the_habits_of_happiness

Teen talk [Audio podcast]. (2019–present). The Fan 104.3. http://podcasts.apple.com/us/podcast/teen-talk-podcast/id1495855831

Turner, E. (Host). (2020, May). Parenting through a pandemic (No. 107) [Audio podcast episode]. In *Speaking of Psychology*. American Psychological Association. http://apa.org/research/action/speaking-of-psychology/parenting-pandemic

Youth Radio [Audio podcast]. (2020–present). YR Media. http://yr.media/category/health

Zucker, B. (Host). (2017, May). Children, loss, and stress (No. 47) [Audio podcast episode]. In *Speaking of Psychology*. American Psychological Association. http://apa.org/research/action/speaking-of-psychology/children-loss

ONLINE RESOURCES

The following websites have information and videos on mood, mental health, mindsets, self-compassion, and confidence.

HARVARD SCHOOL OF PUBLIC HEALTH
health.harvard.edu/blog/
A great resource on health and wellness, including the latest research on mental health.

SELF-COMPASSION.ORG
A great resource for learning how to practice self-compassion. Includes research, information, examples, and guided meditations.

SPACETREATMENT.NET
spacetreatment.net/manual-and-books

Contains a list of useful information and resources relating to parenting kids and teens with anxiety and related disorders.

STOPBULLYING.GOV

A federal government website managed by the U.S. Department of Health and Human Services. Contains useful information relating to bullying in schools, federal laws and civil rights, and cyberbullying.

THE BOUNCE BACK PROJECT: PROMOTING HEALTH THROUGH HAPPINESS

feelinggoodmn.org/what-we-do/bounce-back-project-/

ORGANIZATIONS

THE TREVOR PROJECT

thetrevorproject.org
The largest suicide prevention and crisis intervention organization for LGBTQ young people.

SUICIDE PREVENTION LIFELINE

suicidepreventionlifeline.org
1-800-273-8255
Provides free 24/7 support for people in distress.

DIY AND JOURNALING RESOURCES

If you want more writing prompts, journaling activities, and to practice great self-care at your own pace, these are some of my favorite workbooks.

Gratitude Daily. (2020). *The ultimate middle school gratitude journal: Thinking big and thriving in middle school with 100 days of gratitude, daily journal prompts and inspirational quotes.* Creative Ideas Publishing.

Hutt, R. (2019). *Feeling better: CBT workbook for teens.* Althea Press.

Schwarz, N. (2021, September 7). 15 tips to build self esteem and confidence in teens. *Big Life Journals.* biglifejournal.com/blogs/blog/build-self-esteem-confidence-teens

Pellegrino, M. W., & Sather, K. (2019). *Neon words: 10 brilliant ways to light up your writing.* Magination Press.

MOBILE APPS

Sometimes an app can be just the thing to help guide you through self-soothing, calming, and energizing your mind and body. Here are some that are worth a try and maybe even to recommend to the grown-ups in your life!

CALM
Learn and practice mindfulness with hundreds of calming, breathing, and meditation techniques.

365 GRATITUDE
Daily prompts to help you grow your gratitude mindset and connect with others who are striving to do the same.

HAPPIFY
Learn and practice activities that can help you combat negativity, anxiety, and stress while fostering positive traits like gratitude and empathy.

HEADSPACE

Learn to meditate with guided practices that help you relax, manage stress, and focus your energy to be more centered.

INSIGHT TIMER

Learn to meditate and choose from a wide variety of meditation styles and themes, from music to voice-guided practices.

Acknowledgments

I am grateful beyond words to **Dr. Bonnie Zucker** for bringing me along on this journey. You are the best mentor, teacher, friend, therapist, colleague, life coach, editor that anyone could ask for. Thank you for your endless generosity.

Kristine Enderle—thank you so much for taking a chance on me and for your vision, ideas, effort, and commitment to creating books that I wish I had on my bookcase in middle school.

Julie Spalding—for putting up with all of my edits, even at the last minute, and putting in so much time and effort.

Rachel Ross—for making the book shine and feel so special and personal.

Mat—thank you for cheering me on, always believing in me, and holding down the fort while I wrote. None of this would be possible without you in my life. You inspired me from the very beginning to do what I love and do it my own way without compromise. Love you.

Mom—I quite literally could not run my life (much less write a book!) without you. You embody unconditional love, and it is thanks to you that I can practice what I preach and imperfectly reach towards balance, acceptance, and gratitude.

Katie & Daniela—thank you for always being there, sharing in my excitement, and continuing to teach me about unconditional love and sisterhood. I am grateful that we are all together again and count my lucky stars every day.

Emilyn—thank you for everything you do for us. I could not have written this book without your dedication, time, effort, patience, and calm presence. You always pick up the pieces!

Dad—I feel your presence every day. Thank you for allowing me to always be myself, even during the ups and downs of my teen years, and always making me feel important and loved.

To my teachers, mentors, colleagues, and friends in the field—you continue to help me be a better psychologist (and human), and thus a better writer of this book. Special thank you to **Jess** (friend, sister, therapist, consultant, life coach) and **Maury** (friend, teacher, truth bomber).

BIBLIOGRAPHY

CHAPTER 1

Beck, A. T. (2019). A 60-year evolution of cognitive theory and therapy. *Perspectives on Psychological Science, 14*(1), 16–20. https://doi.org/10.1177%2F1745691618804187

Beck, A. T., & Alford, B. A. (2009). *Depression: Causes and treatments* (2nd ed). University of Pennsylvania Press.

Beck, A. T., & Bredemeier, K. (2016). A unified model of depression: Integrating clinical, cognitive, biological, and evolutionary perspectives. *Clinical Psychological Science, 4*(4), 596–619. https://doi.org/10.1177%2F2167702616628523

Beck, A. T., John, B. K., & Beck, J. (2021). The development of psychiatric disorders from adaptive behavior to serious mental health conditions. *Cognitive Therapy and Research, 45*(2), 385–390. https://psycnet.apa.org/doi/10.1007/s10608-021-10227-3

Gross, J. J. (2002). Emotion regulation: affective, cognitive, and social consequences. *Psychophysiology, 39*(3), 281–291. https://doi.org/10.1017/s0048577201393198

John, O. P., & Gross, J. J. (2004). Healthy and unhealthy emotion regulation: personality processes, individual differences, and life span development. *Journal of Personality, 72*(6), 1301–1333. https://doi.org/ 10.1111/j.1467-6494.2004.00298.x

Lau, J. Y. (2013). *Developmental aspects of mood disorders. Current Topics in Behavioral Neurosciences, 14, 15–27.*
https://doi.org/10.1007/7854_2012_214

Nettle, D., & Bateson, M. (2012). The evolutionary origins of mood and its disorders. *Current Biology, 22*(17), R712–R721.
https://doi.org/10.1016/j.cub.2012.06.020

Oud, M., et al. (2019). Effectiveness of CBT for children and adolescents with depression: A systematic review and meta-regression analysis. *European Journal of Psychiatry.* Apr; 57, 33–45.
https://doi.org/10.1016/j.eurpsy.2018.12.008

Porto, P. R., et al. (2009). Does cognitive behavioral therapy change the brain? A systematic review of neuroimaging in anxiety disorders. *Journal of Neuropsychiatry and Clinical Neuroscience.* PMID: 19622682.
https://doi.org/10.1176/jnp.2009.21.2.114

Stelzig, O., & Sevecke, K. (2019). Coping with Stress During Childhood and Adolescence. *Praxis der Kinderpsychologie und Kinderpsychiatrie, 68*(7), 592–605.

CHAPTER 2

Casey, B. J., Jones, R. M., Levita, L., Libby, V., Pattwell, S. S., Ruberry, E. J., Soliman, F., & Somerville, L. H. (2010). The storm and stress of adolescence: insights from human imaging and mouse genetics. *Developmental Psychobiology, 52*(3), 225–235.
https://dx.doi.org/10.1002%2Fdev.20447

Centers for Disease Control and Prevention. (2021, March 22). Data and statistics on children's mental health.
https://cdc.gov/childrensmentalhealth/data.html

Harvard Health. (2011, March 7). *The adolescent brain: Beyond raging hormones.* https://health.harvard.edu/mind-and-mood/the-adolescent-brain-beyond-raging-hormones

Hazell, P. (2011). *Depression in children and adolescents*. BMJ Clinical Evidence.

Hueston, C. M., Cryan, J. F., & Nolan, Y. M. (2017). Stress and adolescent hippocampal neurogenesis: Diet and exercise as cognitive modulators. *Translational Psychiatry, 7*(4), 1081. https://doi.org/ 10.3389/fnint.2012.00065

Ladouceur, C. D. (2012). Neural systems supporting cognitive-affective interactions in adolescence: The role of puberty and implications for affective disorders. *Frontiers in Integrative Neuroscience, 6*, 65. https://doi.org/10.3389/fnint.2012.00065

National Institute of Mental Health. (2018, February). *Depression*. https://nimh.nih.gov/health/topics/depression

National Institute of Mental Health. (2021, October). *Major depression*. https://nimh.nih.gov/health/statistics/major-depression

Peper, J. S., & Dahl, R. E. (2013). Surging hormones: Brain-behavior interactions during puberty. *Current Directions in Psychological Science, 22*(2), 134–139. https://doi.org/10.1177%2F0963721412473755

Romero, C., Master, A., Paunesku, D., Dweck, C. S., & Gross, J. J. (2014). Academic and emotional functioning in middle school: the role of implicit theories. *Emotion, 14*(2), 227–34. https://doi.org/10.1037/a0035490

Society for Endocrinology. (n.d.). *Hormones*. http://yourhormones.info/hormones

Steinberg, L. (2004). Risk-Taking in Adolescence: What Changes, and Why? *Annals of the New York Academy of Sciences, 1021*, 51–58. https://doi.org/10.1196/annals.1308.005

Steinberg, L. (2005). Cognitive and Affective Development in Adolescence. *Trends in Cognitive Science, 9*(2), 68–75. https://doi.org/10.1016/j.tics.2004.12.005

CHAPTER 3

Caballero, A., Granberg, R., & Tseng, K. Y. (2016). Mechanisms contributing to prefrontal cortex maturation during adolescence. *Neuroscience and Biobehavioral Reviews, 70,* 4–12. https://doi.org/10.1016/j.neubiorev.2016.05.013

Casey, B. J., Heller, A. S., Gee, D. G., & Cohen, A.O. (2019). Development of the emotional brain. *Neuroscience Letters, 693,* 29–34. https://doi.org/10.1016/j.neulet.2017.11.055

Chalah, M. A., & Ayache, S. S. (2018). Disentangling the neural basis of cognitive behavioral therapy in psychiatric disorders: A focus on depression. *Brain Sciences, 8*(8), 150. https://doi.org/10.3390%2Fbrainsci8080150

De Oliveira, R. M. W. (2020). Neuroplasticity. *Journal of Chemical Neuroanatomy, 108,* 101822. https://doi.org/10.1016/j.jchemneu.2020.101822

Diaz-Thomas, A., Anhalt, H., & Solorzano, C. B. (2019, May). *Puberty.* Hormone Health Network. http://hormone.org/diseases-and-conditions/puberty

Drzewiecki, C. M., & Juraska, J. M. (2020). The structural reorganization of the prefrontal cortex during adolescence as a framework for vulnerability to the environment. *Pharmacology, Biochemistry, and Behavior, 199,* 173044. https://doi.org/10.1016/j.pbb.2020.173044

Furst, J. (2020, January2). *Expert Alert: Keep exercising: New study finds it's good for your brain's gray matter.* Mayo Clinic. https://newsnetwork.mayoclinic.org/discussion/keep-exercising-new-study-finds-its-good-for-your-brains-gray-matter/

Gothe, N. P., Khan, I., Hayes, J., Erlenbach, E., & Damoiseaux, J. S. (2019). Yoga effects on brain health: A Systematic Review of the Current Literature. *Brain Plasticity,* 5(1), 105–122. https://doi.org/10.3233%2FBPL-190084

Jadhav, K. S., & Boutrel, B. (2019). Prefrontal cortex development and emergence of self-regulatory competence: The two cardinal features of adolescence disrupted in context of alcohol abuse. *European Journal of Neuroscience,* 50(3), 2274–2281. https://doi.org/10.1111/ejn.14316

Kaczkurkin, A. N., & Foa, E. B. (2015). Cognitive-behavioral therapy for anxiety disorders: an update on the empirical evidence. *Dialogues in Clinical Neuroscience,* 17(3), 337–346. https://dx.doi.org/10.31887%2FDCNS.2015.17.3%2Fakaczkurkin

Masten, A. M. (2004). Regulatory processes, risks, and resilience in adolescent development. *Annals of the New York Academy of Sciences,* 1021, 310–19. https://doi.org/10.1196/annals.1308.036

Otte, C. (2011). Cognitive behavioral therapy in anxiety disorders: Current state of the evidence. *Dialogues in Clinical Neuroscience,* 13(4), 413–421. https://dx.doi.org/10.31887%2FDCNS.2011.13.4%2Fcotte

Rosso, I. M., et al. (2004). Cognitive and emotional components of frontal lobe functioning in childhood and adolescence. *Annals of the New York Academy of Sciences,* 1021, 355–62. https://doi.org/10.1196/annals.1308.045

Sakurai, T., & Gamo, N. J. (2019). Cognitive functions associated with developing prefrontal cortex during adolescence and developmental neuropsychiatric disorders. *Neurobiology of Disease,* 131, 104322. https://doi.org/10.1016/j.nbd.2018.11.007

Sasmita, A. O., Kuruvilla, J., & Ling, A. (2018). Harnessing neuroplasticity: Modern approaches and clinical future. *The International Journal of Neuroscience,* 128(11), 1061–1077. https://doi.org/10.1080/00207454.2018.1466781

Spessot, A. L., et al. (2004). Neuroimaging of developmental psychopathologies: The importance of self-regulatory and neural plastic processes in adolescence. *Annals of the New York Academy of Sciences, 1021,* 86–104. https://doi.org/10.1196/annals.1308.010

Society for Endocrinology. (n.d.). *Hormones.* http://yourhormones.info/hormones

Suzuki, W. (2017, November). *The brain-changing benefits of exercise* [Video]. Ted Conferences. http://ted.com/talks/wendy_suzuki_the_brain_changing_benefits_of_exercise

CHAPTER 4

Anderson, E., & Shivakumar, G. (2013). Effects of exercise and physical activity on anxiety. *Frontiers in Psychiatry, 4,* 27. https://doi.org/10.3389%2Ffpsyt.2013.00027

Bracha, H. S. (2004). Freeze, flight, fight, fright, faint: Adaptationist perspectives on the acute stress response spectrum. *CNS Spectrums, 9*(9), 679–685. https://doi.org/10.1017/s1092852900001954

Buyukdura, J. S., McClintock, S. M., & Croarkin, P. E. (2011). Psychomotor retardation in depression: Biological underpinnings, measurement, and treatment. *Progress in Neuro-Psychopharmacology & Biological Psychiatry, 35*(2), 395–409. http://doi.org/10.1016/j.pnpbp.2010.10.019

Cooney, G. M., Dwan, K., Greig, C. A., Lawlor, D. A., Rimer, J., Waugh, F. R., McMurdo, M., & Mead, G. E. (2013). Exercise for depression. *The Cochrane Database of Systematic Reviews,* (9), CD004366. https://doi.org/10.1002/14651858.CD004366.pub6

Foley, A., Hillier, S., & Barnard, R. (2011). Effectiveness of once-weekly gym-based exercise programs for older adults post discharge from day rehabilitation: A randomized controlled trial. *British Journal of Sports Medicine, 45*(12), 978–986. https://doi.org/10.1136/bjsm.2009.063966

Fritz, K. M., & O'Connor, P. J. (2016). Acute exercise improves mood and motivation in young men with ADHD symptoms. *Medicine and Science in Sports and Exercise, 48*(6), 1153–1160. https://doi.org/10.1249/MSS.0000000000000864

Häfner, M. (2013). When body and mind are talking: Interoception moderates embodied cognition. *Experimental Psychology, 60*(4), 255–259. https://doi.org/10.1027/1618-3169/a000194

Harvard Health. (2021, March 31). *Sour mood getting you down? Get back to nature.* https://health.harvard.edu/mind-and-mood/sour-mood-getting-you-down-get-back-to-nature

Harvard Health. (2019, May 1). *More evidence that exercise can boost mood.* https://health.harvard.edu/mind-and-mood/more-evidence-that-exercise-can-boost-mood

Hogan, C. L., Mata, J., & Carstensen, L. L. (2013). Exercise holds immediate benefits for affect and cognition in younger and older adults. *Psychology and Aging, 28*(2), 587–594. https://dx.doi.org/10.1037%2Fa0032634

Kerage, D., Sloan, E. K., Mattarollo, S. R., McCombe, P. A. (2019). Interaction of neurotransmitters and neurochemicals with lymphocytes. *Journal of Neuroimmunology, 332*, 99–111. https://doi.org/10.1016/j.jneuroim.2019.04.006

Kiverstein, J., & Miller, M. (2015). The embodied brain: Towards a radical embodied cognitive neuroscience. *Frontiers in Human Neuroscience, 9*, 237. https://doi.org/10.3389/fnhum.2015.00237

Mikkelsen, K., Stojanovska, L., Polenakovic, M., Bosevski, M., & Apostolopoulos, V. (2017). Exercise and mental health. *Maturitas, 106*, 48–56. https://doi.org/10.1016/j.maturitas.2017.09.003

Payne, P., & Crane-Godreau, M. A. (2013). Meditative movement for depression and anxiety. *Frontiers in Psychiatry, 4,* 71. https://dx.doi.org/10.3389%2Ffpsyt.2013.00071

Schuch, F. B., Dunn, A. L., Kanitz, A. C., Delevatti, R. S., & Fleck, M. P. (2016). Moderators of response in exercise treatment for depression: A systematic review. *Journal of Affective Disorders, 195,* 40–49. https://doi.org/10.1016/j.jad.2016.01.014

Wilson, A. D., & Golonka, S. (2013). Embodied cognition is not what you think it is. *Frontiers in Psychology, 4,* 58. https://doi.org/10.3389/fpsyg.2013.00058

World Health Organization. (2020, November 26). *Physical Activity.* https://who.int/news-room/fact-sheets/detail/physical-activity

CHAPTER 5

Chin, B., Lindsay, E. K., Greco, C., Brown, K.W., Smyth, J., & Creswell, J.D. *(in press)*. Acceptance skills drive stress resilience in a mindfulness training randomized controlled trial. *Health Psychology.*

Hayes, S. C., Strosahl, K. D. & Wilson, K. G. (2012). *Acceptance and commitment therapy: The process of mindful change.* The Guilford Press.

Henry, J. D., Castellini, J., Moses, E., & Scott, J. G. (2016). Emotion regulation in adolescents with mental health problems. *Journal of Clinical and Experimental Neuropsychology, 38*(2), 197–207. https://doi.org/10.1080/13803395.2015.1100276

Holmqvist Larsson, K., Andersson, G., Stern, H., & Zetterqvist, M. (2020). Emotion regulation group skills training for adolescents and parents: A pilot study of an add-on treatment in a clinical setting. *Clinical Child Psychology and Psychiatry, 25*(1), 141–155. https://doi.org/10.1177/1359104519869782

Kircanski, K., Lieberman, M. D., & Craske, M. G. (2012). Feelings into words: Contributions of language to exposure therapy. *Psychological Science, 23*(10), 1086–1091. https://doi.org/10.1177/0956797612443830

Luoma, J. B., Hayes, S. C., & Walser, R. (2017). *An acceptance and commitment therapy skills training manual for therapists.* New Harbinger.

Nummenmaa, L., Glerean, E., Hari, R., & Hietanen, J. (2014). Bodily maps of emotions. *Proceedings of the National Academy of Sciences, 111*(2), 646–651. https://doi.org/10.1073/pnas.1321664111

Ressler, K. J. (2010). Amygdala activity, fear, and anxiety: Modulation by stress. *Biological Psychiatry, 67*(12), 1117–1119. https://dx.doi.org/10.1016%2Fj.biopsych.2010.04.027

Schumer, M., Lindsay, E. K., & Creswell, J. D. (2018). Brief mindfulness interventions and negative affectivity: A systematic review and meta-analysis. *Journal of Consulting and Clinical Psychology, 86,* 569–583. https://doi.org/10.1037/ccp0000324

Torre, J. B., & Lieberman, M. D. (2018). Putting feelings into words: Affect labeling as implicit emotion regulation. *Emotion Review, 10*(2), 116–124. https://doi.org/10.1177%2F1754073917742706

Williams, J. M. G., Teasdale, J. D., Segal, Z. V., & Kabat-Zinn, J. (2007). *The mindful way through depression: Freeing yourself from chronic unhappiness.* Guilford Press.

Wilms, R., Lanwehr, R., & Kastenmüller, A. (2020). Emotion regulation in everyday life: The role of goals and situational factors. *Frontiers in Psychology, 11.* https://doi.org/10.3389/fpsyg.2020.00877

Zettle, R. D. (2007). ACT for depression. New Harbinger.

University of California, Los Angeles. (2007, June 22). Putting feelings into words produces therapeutic effects in the brain. *ScienceDaily*. https://sciencedaily.com/releases/2007/06/070622090727.htm

CHAPTER 6

Caouette, J. D., & Guyer, A. E. (2016). Cognitive distortions mediate depression and affective response to social acceptance and rejection. *Journal of Affective Disorders*, 190, 792–799. https://doi.org/10.1016/j.jad.2015.11.015

Costantini, I., Kwong, A., Smith, D., Lewcock, M., Lawlor, D. A., Moran, P., Tilling, K., Golding, J., & Pearson, R. M. (2021). Locus of control and negative cognitive styles in adolescence as risk factors for depression onset in young adulthood: Findings from a prospective birth cohort study. *Frontiers in Psychology*, 12. https://doi.org/10.3389/fpsyg.2021.599240

Fazakas-DeHoog, L. L., Rnic, K., & Dozois, D. (2017). A cognitive distortions and deficits model of suicide ideation. *Europe's Journal of Psychology*, 13(2), 178–193. https://doi.org/10.5964%2Fejop.v13i2.1238

Flores, J., Caqueo-Urízar, A., Ramírez, C., Arancio, G., & Cofré, J. P. (2020). Locus of control, self-control, and gender as predictors of internalizing and externalizing problems in children and adolescents in northern Chile. *Frontiers in Psychology*, 11. https://doi.org/10.3389/fpsyg.2020.02015

Gale, C. R., Batty, G. D., & Deary, I. J. (2008). Locus of control at age 10 years and health outcomes and behaviors at age 30 years: The 1970 British Cohort Study. *Psychosomatic Medicine*, 70(4), 397–403. https://doi.org/10.1097/PSY.0b013e31816a719e

Gellatly, R., & Beck, A. T. (2016). Catastrophic thinking: A transdiagnostic process across psychiatric disorders. *Cognitive Therapy and Research, 40*(4), 441–452. https://psycnet.apa.org/doi/10.1007/s10608-016-9763-3

Jenness, J., Jager-Hyman, S., Heleniak, C., Beck, A. T., Sheridan, M. A., & McLaughlin, K. A. (2016). Catastrophizing, rumination, and reappraisal prospectively predict adolescent PTSD symptom onset following a terrorist attack. *Depression and Anxiety, 33*(11), 1039–1047. https://doi.org/10.1002/da.22548

Hofmann, S., Asmundson, G., & Beck, A. T. (2013). The science of cognitive therapy. *Behavior Therapy, 44*(2), 199–212. https://doi.org/10.1016/j.beth.2009.01.007

Hofmann, S. G., Asnaani, A., Vonk, I. J., Sawyer, A. T., & Fang, A. (2012). The efficacy of cognitive behavioral therapy: A review of meta-analyses. *Cognitive Therapy and Research, 36*(5), 427–440. https://doi.org/10.1007%2Fs10608-012-9476-1

Panourgia, C., & Comoretto, A. (2017). Do cognitive distortions explain the longitudinal relationship between life adversity and emotional and behavioral problems in secondary school children? *Stress and Health: Journal of the International Society for the Investigation of Stress, 33*(5), 590–599. https://doi.org/10.1002/smi.2743

Rnic, K., Dozois, D. J., & Martin, R. A. (2016). Cognitive distortions, humor styles, and depression. *Europe's Journal of Psychology, 12*(3), 348–362. https://dx.doi.org/10.5964%2Fejop.v12i3.1118

Young, J. E., Klosko, J. S., & Weishaar, M. (2003). *Schema therapy: A practitioner's guide*. Guilford Publications.

CHAPTER 7

Allen, A. B., & Leary, M. R. (2010). Self-compassion, stress, and coping. *Social and Personality Psychology Compass, 4*(2), 107–118. https://doi.org/10.1111%2Fj.1751-9004.2009.00246.x

Bluth, K., & Eisenlohr-Moul, T. A. (2017). Response to a mindful self-compassion intervention in teens: A within-person association of mindfulness, self-compassion, and emotional well-being outcomes. *Journal of Adolescence, 57*, 108–118. https://doi.org/10.1016/j.adolescence.2017.04.001

Borman, G. D., Rozek, C. S., Pyne, J., & Hanselman, P. (2019). Reappraising academic and social adversity improves middle school students' academic achievement, behavior, and well-being. *Proceedings of the National Academy of Sciences of the United States of America, 116*(33), 16286–16291. https://doi.org/10.1073/pnas.1820317116

Bounce Back Project. (n.d.) *Resilience is made up of five pillars: self-awareness, mindfulness, self-care, positive relationships & purpose.* https://bouncebackproject.org/resilience/

Breines, J. G., & Chen, S. (2012). Self-compassion increases self-improvement motivation. *Personality and Social Psychology Bulletin, 38*(9), 1133–1143. https://doi.org/10.1177%2F0146167212445599

Duckworth, A. (2018). *Grit: The power of passion and perseverance.* Scribner.

Dweck, C. (2007). *Mindset: The new psychology of success.* Ballantine Books.

Helmstetter, S. (2017). *What to say when you talk to yourself: Powerful new techniques to program your potential for success!* Gallery Books.

Neff, K. (n.d.). *About Dr. Kristin Neff.* Self-Compassion. https://self-compassion.org/about/

Neff, K., & Germer, C. (2019, January 29). *The Transformative Effects of Mindful Self-Compassion.* Mindful. https://mindful.org/the-transformative-effects-of-mindful-self-compassion/

Neff, K. D., Kirkpatrick, K. L., & Rude, S. S. (2007). Self-compassion and adaptive psychological functioning. *Journal of Research in Personality, 41,* 139–154. https://doi.org/10.1016/j.jrp.2006.03.004

Machado, A. (n.d.). *Trust in emergence: Grounded theory and my research process.* Brené Brown, LLC. https://brenebrown.com/the-research/

Seppala, E. (2014, May 8). *The scientific benefits of self-compassion.* Stanford Medicine. http://ccare.stanford.edu/uncategorized/the-scientific-benefits-of-self-compassion-infographic/

Stevens, L., Gauthier-Braham, M., & Bush, B. (2018, June 22). *The brain that longs to care for itself: The current neuroscience of self-compassion.* Science Direct. https://sciencedirect.com/science/article/pii/B9780128098370000040

Szasz, A. (2016, May 23). *Self-Compassion with Kristin Neff & Brené Brown.* Brave Therapy. https://bravetherapy.com/self-compassion-with-kristin-neff-brene-brown/

CHAPTER 8

Belli, A., & Carrillat, F., & Zlatevska, N., & Cowley, E. (2021). The wellbeing implications of maximizing: A conceptual framework and meta-analysis. *Journal of Consumer Psychology.* Forthcoming.

Bluth, K., & Blanton, P. W. (2015). The influence of self-compassion on emotional well-being among early and older adolescent males and females. *The Journal of Positive Psychology, 10*(3), 219–230. https://dx.doi.org/10.1080%2F17439760.2014.936967

Brown, B. (2010). *The gifts of imperfection*. Hazelden Publishing.

Crocker, J., Luhtanen, R. K., Cooper, M. L., & Bouvrette, A. (2003). Contingencies of self-worth in college students: Theory and measurement. *Journal of Personality and Social Psychology, 85*(5), 894–908. https://doi.org/10.1037/0022-3514.85.5.894

Hewitt, P., Flett, G., & Mikail, S. (2017). *Perfectionism: A relational approach to conceptualization, assessment, and treatment*. Guilford Press.

Orth, U., Robins, R.W., & Widaman, K.F. (2012). Life-span development of self-esteem and its effects on important life outcomes. *Journal of Personality & Social Psychology, 102*,(6), 1271–1288. https://doi.org/10.1037/a0025558

Sandberg, S., & Grant, A. (2017). *Option b: Facing adversity, building resilience, and finding joy*. Knopf.

Stankov, L., Morony, S., & Lee, Y. P. (2014). Confidence: The best non-cognitive predictor of academic achievement? *Educational Psychology, 34*(1), 9–28. https://doi.org/10.1080/01443410.2013.814194

Vealey, R. S. (2009). Confidence in sport. In Brewer, B.W. (Ed.), *Handbook of sports medicine & science: Sport psychology* (pp. 43–52). Wiley-Blackwell.

CHAPTER 9

Bauer, C. C. C., Caballero, C., Scherer, E., West, M. R., Mrazek, M. D., Phillips, D. T., Whitfield-Gabrieli, S., & Gabrieli, J. D. E. (2019). Mindfulness training reduces stress and amygdala reactivity to fearful faces in middle-school children. *Behavioral Neuroscience, 133*(6), 569–585. https://doi.org/10.1037/bne0000337

Bradley, C. (2021, November 5). *3 ways to improve your gut-brain connection (and mood)*. Mindful. https://mindful.org/3-ways-to-improve-your-gut-brain-connection-and-your-mood/

Centers for Disease Control and Prevention. (2020, September 10). *Sleep in middle and high school students.* https://cdc.gov/healthyschools/features/students-sleep.htm

Chowdhury, M. A. (2021, August 12). *The science & psychology of goal-setting 101.* Positive Psychology. https://positivepsychology.com/goal-setting-psychology/

Clear, J. (2018). *Atomic habits: An easy & proven way to build good habits & break bad ones.* Avery.

Collado, A. (2021). *Behavioral activation for depression: Roots, science, and real-world application* [presentation]. Alvord, Baker, & Associates.

Cramer, S., & Inkster, B. (2017). *Status of mind: Social media and young people's mental health and wellbeing.* Royal Society for Public Health. https://rsph.org.uk/static/uploaded/d125b27c-0b62-41c5-a2c0155a8887cd01.pdf

Harvard Health. (2014, July 16). *What meditation can do for your mind, mood, and health.* https://health.harvard.edu/staying-healthy/what-meditation-can-do-for-your-mind-mood-and-health-

Harvard Health. (2021, March 31). *Sour mood getting you down? Get back to nature.* https://health.harvard.edu/mind-and-mood/sour-mood-getting-you-down-get-back-to-nature

Jacobson, N. S., Martell, C. R., & Dimidjian, S. (2001). Behavioral activation treatment for depression: Returning to contextual roots. *Clinical Psychology: Science and Practice, 8*(3), 255–270. https://doi.org/10.1093/clipsy.8.3.255

Johns Hopkins Medicine. (n.d.). *Teenagers and sleep: How much sleep is enough?* https://hopkinsmedicine.org/health/wellness-and-prevention/teenagers-and-sleep-how-much-sleep-is-enough

Lo, J. C., Ong, J. L., Leong, R. L., Gooley, J. J., & Chee, M. W. (2016). Cognitive performance, sleepiness, and mood in partially sleep deprived adolescents: The need for sleep study. *Sleep, 39*(3), 687–698. https://doi.org/10.5665%2Fsleep.5552

Martell, C. R. (n.d). *Behavioral activation therapy.* https://christophermartell.com/ba.php

Martell, C. R., Addis, M. E., & Jacobson, N. S. (2001). *Depression in context: Strategies for guided action.* W. W. Norton & Co.

Martell, C. R., Dimidjian, S., & Herman-Dunn. (2010). *Behavioral activation for depression.* The Guilford Press.

Murphy, M. (2018, April 15). *Neuroscience explains why you need to write down your goals if you actually want to achieve them.* Forbes. https://forbes.com/sites/markmurphy/2018/04/15/neuroscience-explains-why-you-need-to-write-down-your-goals-if-you-actually-want-to-achieve-them/

Scholey, A., & Owen, L. (2013). Effects of chocolate on cognitive function and mood: A systematic review. *Nutrition reviews, 71*(10), 665–681. https://doi.org/10.1111/nure.12065

Shapiro, D., Cook, I. A., Davydov, D. M., Ottaviani, C., Leuchter, A. F., & Abrams, M. (2007). Yoga as a complementary treatment of depression: Effects of traits and moods on treatment outcome. *Evidence-Based Complementary and Alternative Medicine, 4*(4), 493–502. https://doi.org/10.1093/ecam/nel114

Sharma, A., Madaan, V., & Petty, F. D. (2006). Exercise for mental health. *Primary Care Companion to the Journal of Clinical Psychiatry, 8*(2), 106. http://doi.org/10.4088/PCC.v08n0208a

Short, M. A., & Chee, M. (2019). Adolescent sleep restriction effects on cognition and mood. *Progress in Brain Research, 246,* 55–71. https://doi.org/10.1016/bs.pbr.2019.02.008

Suni, E. (2021, November 22). *Teens and sleep: An overview of why teens face unique sleep challenges and tips to help them sleep better.* https://sleepfoundation.org/teens-and-sleep

Tello, M. (2020, January 29). *Diet and Depression*. Harvard Health. https://health.harvard.edu/blog/diet-and-depression-2018022213309

Weinstein, E. C., & Selman, R. L. (2014). Digital stress: Adolescents' personal accounts. *New Media & Society, 18*(3), 391–409. https://doi.org/10.1177%2F1461444814543989

CHAPTER 10

Hoferichter, F., Kulakow, S., & Hufenbach, M. C. (2021). Support from parents, peers, and teachers is differently associated with middle school students' well-being. *Frontiers in Psychology, 12*, 758226. https://doi.org/10.3389/fpsyg.2021.758226

Lack, C. W., & Green, A. L. (2009). Mood disorders in children and adolescents. *Journal of Pediatric Nursing, 24*(1), 13–25. https://doi.org/10.1016/j.pedn.2008.04.007

Mayo Clinic (2021, October 29). *Mood disorders: Symptoms and causes*. https://mayoclinic.org/diseases-conditions/mood-disorders/symptoms-causes/syc-20365057

National Institute of Mental Health (2021). *What is depression?* https://nimh.nih.gov/health/publications/depression

Rakofsky, J., & Rapaport, M. (2018). Mood disorders: Continuum. *Behavioral Neurology and Psychiatry, 24*(3), 804–827. https://doi.org/10.1212/CON.0000000000000604

Tores, F. (2000, October). *What is depression?* American Psychiatric Association. https://psychiatry.org/patients-families/depression/what-is-depression

ABOUT THE AUTHOR

LENKA GLASSMAN, PsyD, is a licensed psychologist specializing in the treatment of anxiety and related conditions. She runs a private practice in Washington, DC, and Bethesda, MD, where she works with children, teens, adults, and families on issues related to anxiety, obsessive-compulsive disorder, and self-esteem. In addition to her clinical training and career in psychology, Dr. Glassman has worked as a group fitness leader for over 18 years, and views physical exercise as an important component in overall psychological well-being. She lives in Bethesda, MD.

Visit drlenkaglassman.com and @drlenkaglassman on Facebook, Twitter, and Instagram.

ABOUT THE ILLUSTRATOR

DEANDRA HODGE is an illustrator and designer based in Washington, DC. She received her Bachelor of Arts in Fine Arts, concentrating in Graphic Design from University of Montevallo.

Visit @deandrahodge_ on Instagram.